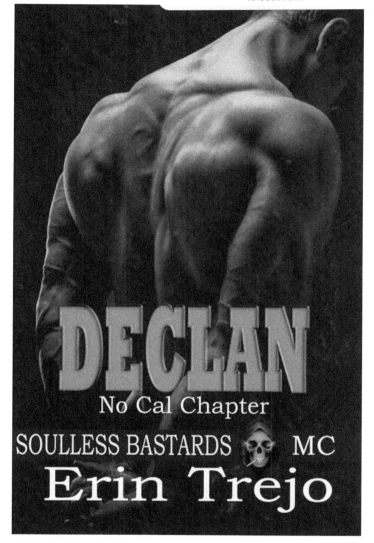

DECLAN

No Cal Chapter

SOULLESS BASTARDS MC

Erin Trejo

Declan

Soulless Bastards MC
NoCal

Declan

Soulless Bastards MC

NoCal

By Erin Trejo

Edited by: Elfwerks Editing

Cover by: Erin Trejo

Cover photos: iStock

Contents

Prologue

"Take the fuckin' gun, boy!" my father roars in my ear. I stick my hand out and grab it. The heaviness is weighing my arm down.

"He took your momma away from you, boy. What are you gonna do about it?" my dad whispers. His overwhelming presence behind me is causing my hand to shake.

"You don't have to do this! Not in front of my girls, Mack, please!" The sheriff cries from his place on his knees, glaring up at my dad. He sits in front of me, his eyes full of tears, two little girls hovering at his side.

"Did you stop when my boy cried for his momma? Did you stop when he yelled?" my dad roars at him. His body is vibrating with rage and anger.

Two years ago, the sheriff killed my mom. We were walking home from the store. She was wearing her cut, the one saying she was the property of Mack, Soulless Bastards MC. He knew who she was. He didn't care. She wore that patch, and she was a target - that's just the way it was back then. He pulled the trigger and killed her. At the young age of twelve, I held her bloody body as she laid there dying in my arms. It killed me inside. My childhood was stolen from me in that moment, forcing me to grow up in the matter of seconds. It forced me to look at myself and who I truly was.

"Come on, Mack! She was armed!" the prick cries.

"Armed? With what? A goddamn grocery bag!" he growls. "No, you knew she was mine. You hated it. Kill him, boy," my dad says as he nudges me forward.

I raise the gun and hold it to his head. My heart stammers in my chest. I've been a prospect for a year now. Fifteen years old and I'm waiting to be just what my father is - the fucking king of it all. The choice was never really mine to begin with being born into this life.

I pull the trigger and watch as the asshole who killed my mother falls to his death. The funny thing is, I don't feel bad about it. At least not in the moment. The little girls cry and scream, throwing themselves over his body. My dad and the guys all holler and cheer for what I've just done, what they put me in the position to do.

"We don't have no one else!" The older of the two looks up at me.

I kneel down in front of her and ask, "How old are you?"

She wipes her eyes on her sleeve. "Seven."

I blow out a breath and pull the rosary over my head. I look down at it, letting the ghosts of my past go. I pass it to her, squeezing it into her hand.

"This will protect you," I tell her softly.

She looks down at it before bringing her eyes back to mine. "What will keep you safe now?"

"I don't need it. I'll be okay." I shove off the ground and walk back over to my dad and the guys.

When I turn and look over my shoulder, her eyes are still on me. I wink at her before walking back to the clubhouse like nothing happened. Like I didn't just kill a man in cold blood in front of his kids.

My chest feels heavy. Her little eyes will forever be burned into my memory.

DECLAN

SOULLESS BASTARDS MC

NoCal

Chapter 1

Brooke

"Fuck off, Ryan!" I yell as our bouncer annoys the hell out of me. I swear to God if that man doesn't leave me alone, I will fire his ass. After I kill him. He's obnoxious.

"You fucking love me, Brooke!" he yells as he walks the other way. Love? Yeah, I don't think so.

"You know he only does it to get you hot," Angel, my sister, says.

I shake my head before smiling at her. "No, he wants to see if I kick his ass." I walk toward the office, letting out a sigh as I leave her behind in the hallway.

I have way too much to get done and not enough time to do it. I don't know why I agreed to help my uncle with his damn strip club, of all things. I'm not a stripper, and I'd probably prove to be a better bouncer than I would working in this goddamn office. Yet, here I am doing the family thing. I guess a part of me feels that I owe my uncle for taking care of me and my sister when we were younger.

"Brooke!" I hear her voice and shake my head. It's too early in the day to deal with Ashley. I just can't do it. The door flies open and in walks the girl who has been my best friend since I was three. Ashley is almost as close to me as my own sister.

"My house. Tonight. Ellen and her girls are coming. It's a sleepover sort of thing." I close my eyes before banging my head on my desk. Literally. Yes, she drives me that insane.

"Stop that!" she yells.

"I love you, Ash, but I'm not coming. Ellen is the most self-centered bitch I've ever met," I say, pulling my head back up.

"She is, but she also brings alcohol. You are coming. You live across the street, Brooke! You don't want her at your house, do you? I'll bring her over. You know I will." She crosses her arms and flips her long blonde hair over her shoulder.

"We're twenty-two years old, Ash. We are too old for sleepovers," I remind her. She doesn't care. She's a kid at heart, and I'm pretty sure she always will be. That's one of the things I like about her - she keeps me grounded.

"Whatever. Don't come and see if I don't sit on your damn doorstep with her," she says before turning and leaving the room. Why is she my best friend? Oh, yeah. She's always there when I need her, and I love the bitch.

I pull out all the paperwork I have to get through today and get started when I hear my uncle.

"Let me catch you snorting one more thing and see if I don't fire your ass!" my uncle yells over his shoulder as he walks in, his gaze haunted. He always looks that way these days. The club is getting the best of him, and I can't say that I don't understand. It's a mess.

"You look tired," I say before getting back to the paperwork at hand.

"Tired? Dead is more like it. Half the fucking girls here are using. We need new talent. We need more money. Shit, Brooke." He drops into the chair in front of me before I sigh and look up. He's defeated, and I know how that feels.

"I'm trying to figure out the money part. We can cut some of the budget with cheaper beer. As far as the girls, I don't know what to do there. I can't stand half of them." He nods his head, knowing that it's true. I think most of them are skanks, and they don't follow the fucking rules. If they'd stop fucking half the clients for free and dance for their money, we wouldn't have this problem.

"I'm glad you're here, Brooke. I really am. There's no way in hell that I'd want to ask my brother Darren for any help with this place. That would for sure be the end of the club," my Uncle Devon says.

I nod once. I'm sort of glad I'm here. I missed being around family. I liked my life the way it was, but I didn't have any goals for myself. I was basically living day to day off my savings. I did work at one point for a local photographer. That didn't last long though.

"Me too, Uncle D."

"Drinks tonight?" he asks, standing from his chair.

"No, I'm stuck with Ashley and her hoard of uptight bitches." He laughs before leaving the room. Too bad I'm not that excited. I drag out my trusty pen and start going over all the shit paperwork, hoping I can figure out a way to get my uncle's club back in the green. He's let the club fall so far into the red it's nearly a lost cause; I don't know if I will be able to pull him out.

"What the hell am I doing here?" I grumble as my eyes begin to cross.

Chapter 2

Declan

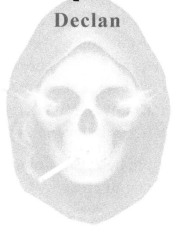

I feel like my eyes are about to burst out of my head. I'm not an office man; I'm a goddamn biker. If there was anyone less qualified to be looking over this shit, it's me. We run guns and drugs. You may think that doesn't involve a lot of math and shit, but you'd be surprised. I'm just not the one to work those numbers.

"Blu, why the fuck you got me over here lookin' at this shit?" I finally give up and ask. It's way out of my fucking league. I don't do numbers unless I'm counting how many girls I'm taking to bed.

"'Cause I know that motherfucker was skimmin' money off the top. I just want a second pair of eyes on it before I blow his goddamn head off." Blu blows out a puff of smoke, making me laugh. He's been ready to kill Chop for a while now. This just gives him the justification he needs to do it.

I glance back down at the pile of papers in front of me before I raise my eyebrows and say, "Well, I think you have enough evidence to blow his head off. Whoever you vote in here has a shit ton of work to catch up on. Don't look like he did shit for the last six months but take the club's money." I lean back in the chair and sigh as Blu paces the room. He's on edge, and I can't blame him.

"I suppose I should thank fuck we're partyin' tonight. If we can fuckin' afford it!"

I let out a chuckle. Blu has been so amped up for the last few days since learning about what Chop was up to. I haven't seen him this fucking fidgety in years.

"We got this handled, Uncle Blu." He looks over, his dark gray eyes mimicking mine. "Yeah, I know. It's just hard when it's a fuckin' brother, ya know?"

I nod my head. I do agree there. There's nothing worse than when one of your brothers does shit that is unacceptable to the club. Stealing from

7

us? That's a death sentence, and we all know it. There are times that you sit and think that maybe they had good reason to do what they did, but in the end, all they had to do was ask. We're all family here.

"I hear you. Let's just get this party over with and then we'll handle Chop. You got Griz comin' in for that shit?" I ask, grabbing a cigarette of my own. I light it up as I take in my uncle. He took over this club years ago when my father was killed. He got into a war with another club outside of our territory. No one ever figured out what the hell he was doing over there to begin with. It wasn't club business, that much we know. We always knew my uncle would be president. I'm ok in my VP spot. One day this shit will be mine, though. I know Blu likes to think one of his boys will take over, but Mayhem is so far out of his head, no one would vote that motherfucker in. His other son Tic's happy being a soldier. He doesn't want to take the reins. He doesn't want the extra stress that comes with being in charge.

"Yeah, he'll be in next weekend if shit pans out. I just don't know that I can keep my shit together until then," he says.

I chuckle, knowing just how fucking hard that is. When you know you have a thief in the club, you want to handle it.

"Let's go get this shit set up. I gotta run up to the store for a few things," I say, shoving myself out of the chair. Blu nods his head and follows me out into the main room.

This clubhouse is old - it's been here for years. I come from a long line of Soulless Bastards. My dad, uncle, and grandpa before them were part of the club. Hell, the Bastards date back into the sixties. The clubhouse has stood through it all. Just like it was made to do.

"Yo! Dec! Check this shit out," Mayhem yells as I leave the office. I watch the crazy son of a bitch as he lights up the four joints hanging between his lips.

"What the fuck are you doin'?" I ask with my hands planted on my hips. He has clearly lost his shit today.

"Gettin' ready to party. You want some?" he asks. I shake my head and walk out the side door to see what all the girls have set up.

"You need help out here?" I ask Prim, knowing the only help she's in need of is a dick between her thighs. That girl is downright hateful.

She's a club whore who has been around since she was born. She's more of a sister to most of us, though.

"Do I look like I need help? Go ask Cherry. You know she can't do shit for herself." She flips her long blonde hair over her shoulder before arranging the napkins on the table. I swear to God that girl needs one good fuck. Maybe that would make her less of a bitch. Who the hell knows, might make her worse. I don't know what she's doing with those damn prospects when she clearly needs a real man. But that's not my problem.

"Cherry Bear. You need help?" I ask over her shoulder when I walk up behind her. Her blue eyes come to meet mine, a smile curling her lips. I turn and bend over to grab the box off the ground and set it on the table when I hear her moan.

"You checkin' out my ass?" I ask her with a grin on my face.

"It is a nice ass," she says.

"You might be grabbin' onto it later." I swat her on the ass before helping her pull the rest of the napkins and plates from the box.

God, I love being VP. I love being a Soulless Bastard.

Chapter 3

Brooke

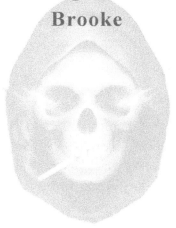

"Ok! Everyone shut up!" Ash yells at the rest of the girls. I feel like a fucking idiot. I feel like we are having some sort of fucked up high school flashback. The only difference is I didn't have this many friends in high school; I only had Ash and my sister. Sad truth.

"Ok. Truth or dare?" Ashley says, looking at Ellen. I roll my eyes knowing she will take truth. The uptight princess claims to do no wrong. Why am I here again?

"Truth," she says, her squeaky little voice grating on my last nerve. I pull my phone out and check my messages. Oh look, there are none! Big fucking surprise.

"Did you really suck Jimmy off in the bathroom at your work?" Ashley asks leaning forward. Ashley's had a crush on this Jimmy idiot since we were in high school, although no one knows it but me.

"Eww, no!" Ellen squeals. "He has a thing for one of the girls in editing. She's a total slut. She has screwed almost everyone in the building. I think that's how she got the editing job anyway. She probably screwed the boss." Ellen continues to ramble on as I let my mind drift off.

I have to figure out a way to get the club back on track. My uncle's life revolves around that club. He put every cent he ever made back into it, I'd hate to see him lose it now.

"Excuse me. Hello!" Ashley says as she waves her hand in my face. "It's your turn. Truth or dare?"

"Dare," I say, watching the smile curl her lips.

"There's a biker club down the street. I dare you to go over there and get a beer from one of them." The other girls all gasp and clap their hands like a bunch of damn fools. I roll my eyes, grab my chucks, and zip up my sweatshirt.

"Can I put on my jeans or do I go like this?" I ask, pointing down to my little booty shorts I wore as pajamas.

"No, you can go like that." Ashley giggles. She's such a bitch. And I love her.

"Don't do that. They are bad people." Ellen covers her mouth before Ashley says, "It's ok. Brooke knows self-defense." I roll my eyes. Self-defense? That's putting it lightly. I head toward the door when they all press their faces to the window to watch me.

The air is cooler tonight, and I can hear the music blasting from the clubhouse. We all know it's there. It's been there for years. The neighborhood doesn't complain about it partially because they are afraid of them. I'm not. Never have been, but then again, I've never been down near their clubhouse either. At the end of the block is when I see it come into view. It's out of place in the middle of this little neighborhood, but from the stories I've been told, it's been here since the sixties. I see a guy that looks to be in his twenties standing by the gate, a cigarette hanging from his lips and a beer in his hand.

"Can a girl get one of those?" I ask as I approach, his eyes coming to meet mine. A slow grin creeps across his face as he looks my body up and down.

"What is it you're wantin'?" He grabs his dick with his free hand.

"The beer, playboy." I nod to the drink in his hand. He raises his eyebrow before passing it to me. I take a pull from the bottle before I slowly run my tongue around the rim, dipping it inside. I pull it free with a pop just as another man walks up.

"Prospect!" he snaps. He's a little pissed. The kid in front of me straightens up before looking over at the man. He's tall and wide. I can see the way his t-shirt clings to every muscle of his body. His long dark shaggy hair hangs around his shoulders in a sexy way.

"What has your interest?" the man asks while eyeing the guy up and down.

"She was just askin' for a beer," the prospect says, nodding at me.

"Is that so?" His eyes turn to me, and my heart leaps a little. His gray eyes are penetrating and hard as he studies my face. "What is your job right now, Prospect?" the bigger guy asks while his eyes run up and down my body. I knew I should have put on fucking pants!

"Lookout, Declan."

The guy nods once before he says, "Get the fuck back inside and send me out Mouse!" The kid visibly jumps before heading back inside the gate.

"I'll just go," I say softly as I point over my shoulder, not wanting to cause any more trouble for the kid than I already have.

"No, you won't," his gruff voice says.

Oh, well shit! What makes me stop and stand here? I have no fucking clue! It could be the sexy sound of his voice or that I'm a complete fool, but either way, I stand here.

"I don't think I have to take orders from some muscled-up brooding jackass," I snap. For some reason, his bossiness is annoying me. His eyes roam over my face making me slightly uneasy.

"You're a mouthy little thing. I'd like to see how you can use those lips you keep movin'." My heart kicks up a notch. He wouldn't dare.

"Yeah. That's not going to happen, caveman. I'm leaving." I start to turn when he stops me yet again.

"Not yet, darlin'. I'm not done with you."

Chapter 4

Declan

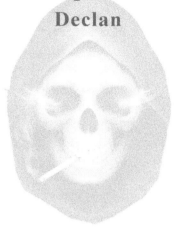

Her body is hot as fuck. Her tits are big and round, sticking out of the top of her jacket. Her lips look utterly fuckable. My dick jerks as I take her in.

"Excuse me?" she asks with a slight attitude.

"I said, you ain't leavin' yet. I need a favor." I smile at her. She looks around before Mouse steps out of the gate.

"You wanted me, Dec?" he asks looking up at me.

"Yeah. Your friend there couldn't handle his duty. Does this girl here distract you, Mouse?" I demand, nodding at the girl.

Mouse looks at her and then back up and down the road before he says, "Not in the slightest. Am I on lookout?"

I give him a nod, but the girl just stands there with her mouth hanging open. I look down at the her before I ask, "Where did you come from?" She pulls her attention from Mouse and drags her eyes back to mine.

"I live down the road. We ran out of beer." As quickly as she looked surprised, she has her game face back on. I like that.

"The store not an option?" I ask. She looks stunned for a second.

"It was a dare," she finally mumbles. "I'm leaving," she adds, her cheeks turning pink with embarrassment. She turns on her heel and starts to walk away.

"Yo, Mouse. If anyone looks for me, tell them I walked this pretty little thing home," I say. The girl jumps before looking at me again. Yeah, I'm walking her ass home.

"I got here on my own; I think I'll be fine," she says with her sassy little attitude. I think I might like it. I throw my arm around her shoulders and walk. I don't give her a chance to respond or react. She damn well better follow if she knows what's good for her. She doesn't look up at me as we walk down the road. It's a strange feeling to be walking out here without any of the guys. I don't typically come out this way, no reason to do so. The main road is out the other way.

"Which house?" I ask when she starts to slow down.

She inclines her head toward the house in front of us. "This one." I look up to find a group of women staring out the window with their mouths open. Only one makes a move to come outside.

"Brooke, I said to get a beer, not the biker." She grins at her friend. I have to chuckle at that one.

"I did," she says with pride as she holds up the bottle. I snatch it out of her hand and take a long pull.

"So, you ladies havin' a good night?" I ask. The blonde just stares at me like I'm a fucking mirage.

"It's great. Thanks for walking me back," the dark-haired girl I now know as Brooke says.

"Let me explain a few things to you girls," I say with a steely calm as I take down what's left of the beer. I throw the bottle at the side of the house, watching it shatter. The girls all jump, clearly frightened by me. Why not take it a little further? Let them know exactly who they are dealing with. I pull the gun from the back of my jeans, stepping up to Brooke's side. I slowly bring the gun up and hold it up to her throat.

"My boys over at the clubhouse would rip you girls to shreds. In fact, I think they would enjoy it." I slide the gun down between her tits, but I don't stop there. No, I keep going. I want to see what kind of reaction I get out of them.

"If I catch any of you comin' to my motherfuckin' gate just one more time, I will unleash the boys on you." Sliding the gun down between her legs, I toy with her pussy with it. The other girl gasps but this one? Brooke? I think she just fucking moaned. What the hell is with this girl? She isn't going to fight me? My dick jerks as Blondie speaks. "We won't bother you again, sir. I'm so sorry," she apologizes quickly in a timid voice.

"I don't know that I agree with that," Brooke chimes in with a determined tone to her voice. The harder I grind the gun between her legs, the more I think I'm turning her on. Fuck me!

"Blondie, go inside," I growl. She jolts but does as she's told. In fact, she does it quickly, leaving her friend to fend for herself. I spin Brooke in my arms, looking into her eyes.

"What the fuck is wrong with you? You got some kind of fetish that you want fulfilled?" I ask, showing her the gun.

"No, not really. I just like the feel of hard steel between my thighs."

Fuck! Now my dick is standing straight up and ready to take her pussy like I'm sure she's never been taken before. She's a mouthy little girl, but I have to wonder if she's ever had a real man between those thighs. Our eyes dance, hers with lust and mine with danger. She leans into me slightly. Her lips slowly part. I'm torn as to what I should do. Walk away from her and leave her breathless? Or take her right here and now? She doesn't know the kind of person she's fucking with right now.

Chapter 5

Brooke

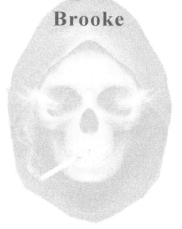

Our standoff is getting heated. His blaze with a fire that I want to touch.

"You've lost your goddamn mind, girl," he says but slides the gun down my chest once more. I think he likes it just as much as I do. His gun keeps moving as his eyes burn into mine. When it slips between my legs again, I part them slightly. His eyes go wide. He licks his lips.

"You like this, butterfly?" he asks, his eyes slowly moving over the butterfly necklace hanging around my neck. I nod once, loving the way it feels. The heat that spreads through my body, the way he works me with that gun. I should be scared shitless of guns after what happened to my dad, but I'm not. I'm oddly turned on by them.

"Would you let me do it?" he asks, his eyes peering at me through hooded lids.

"Do what?" I ask, nearly to my breaking point.

"Let me fuck you with this gun?" The sexual way he says it has my pussy clenching. I nod slowly before he backs me up against the side of the house. My back hits the hard wall before he slides my shorts to the side. He looks down at me, his breath inches from my skin. "Spread 'em."

I part my legs wider as he brings the gun to his mouth. He slides it in, getting it slick with his spit before lowering it between my legs and slowly sliding it inside of me. My body responds. Declan, that's what the guy called him, works it in and out of me. His eyes stay on mine the whole time. He doesn't even flinch as he fucks my body with his gun. I tilt my head back as heat floods my body. It's wild, it's scary, and it's sexy as fuck!

"Do it," he grumbles.

I let go, I explode, cumming all over the barrel of this man's gun and I feel no fucking shame for it. Declan eases the gun out of me before lifting it to his lips once more. His body seems taut with tension. I watch him suck the end into his mouth, tasting me. When he pops it free, I almost come again. Declan reaches down adjusting the apparent hard-on that he's sporting. He is clearly enjoying what he's doing to me.

"Don't come around my fuckin' clubhouse," he says in a pissed off tone before turning and walking away. My body wants more. So, much more. I want to touch him. I want to feel his muscles ripple beneath my fingers as he fucks me. I want to feel exactly what he has in those jeans. I step out from next to the house to find Ashley standing there in shock.

"Are you ok?" she asks. I nod as I watch the man who just gun fucked me walk away. His hand runs through his hair as he goes. He glances over his shoulder but stops when he sees me watching him.

His eyes are on fire. His gaze is heated as we stand here with our eyes connected, licking his lips before Ashley grabs my arm and tugs me back toward the door. I keep my eyes on him until she drags me into the house.

"That was the shittiest dare ever," she says. I follow her up the steps and back into the house. The other girls are packing up their stuff. My mouth falls open, and a little laugh escapes.

"What are you doing?" I ask trying to keep myself from the explosive laughter that wants to erupt.

"We're leaving. This neighborhood is revolting. I can't even believe I came over here," Ellen whines as she shoves her stuff into a bag. I laugh before turning and stepping back out onto the porch. That's when I really lose it. I laugh until my sides hurt.

When the laughter becomes too much, I slide down and sit on the step as I look at the spot in the middle of the road. The memory of what happened there quickly halting all my laughter. There's nothing there, at least not anymore. Just the memory and the heartache. The last memory I have of my father when his life was so brutally taken from us.

My heart never felt the same after that. I saw it all. I was only thankful that Angel was too young to remember. I reach into my sweatshirt pocket and run my fingers over the rosary, letting the heavy weight of the cross linger in my palm. It was so long ago, yet the memory is so vivid it feels like it happened yesterday. The way my father begged. The bullet that ended it all.

The boy who gave me the rosary.

Chapter 6

Declan

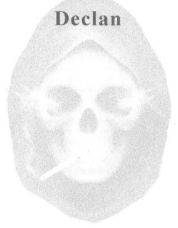

"Where the hell have you been?" Mayhem yells when I walk through the gates with a shit eating grin on my face.

"What the fuck you care?" I ask playfully as I walk past him and straight for the cooler. I need a goddamn beer after what she just let me do to her. In fact, I need a few.

I pop the top off and watch the rest of the guys having a good time. Tic's over there rubbing up on some girl, half his dick hanging from his jeans.

Blu is watching Kenderly like a fucking hawk. I wonder what the fucking deal is with them.

Kenderly is the daughter of a club member, Hawk. He was sent to prison a year ago. I don't think we will be seeing him for a while, but his daughter stuck around. She grew up here. She's one of us.

"What the fuck is goin' on there?" Dread, one of my brothers, asks when he gets closer to me.

I follow his gaze to the crowd that's hanging around the far table before I say, "Fuck if I know. Let's go find out."

We stroll over to the table to find Cherry dancing on it. That girl is all kinds of crazy, but you have to love it. I tip my beer up to my lips while I watch the show in front of me. The way she sways her hips, pulling the little strings of her top. She's hot as hell, and I'd like nothing more than to have her lips wrapped around my dick right now.

"She's fuckin' hot, man." Dread slaps a hand against my chest. I nod, agreeing with him. That she is.

"Hey, Dec. Come on; we need to talk." I glance over my shoulder to see Chop. Fuck, I didn't want to have to deal with this shit tonight. Chop has been a good friend, but the fact is, he's a

26

fucking traitor. He's a traitor to this club and me. I take one last look at Cherry as she bends over, showing everything she has to offer to the crowd. The guys roar and chant.

I follow along behind Chop before he stops near the door.

"What's up?" I ask not, really wanting to hear the answer. I can see the look on his face. He has to know that we know something's up.

"I need to ask you somethin', brother to brother," he says, his gaze locking with mine. Shit! Here it comes.

"What's that?" I ask as I lean against the wall, crossing my arm over my chest.

"A few of the prospects have been talkin'. They said shit with the Evil Claws is gettin' worse." I narrow my gaze at him. That's what the fuck he has been worried about?

I shake my head before I say, "Prospects need to mind their goddamn business. They don't know shit because there isn't shit to know. You think we'd leave the brothers out of somethin' like that, Chop?" I ask, pulling away from the wall. That's really pissed me off now. His lack of trust in his own club is his concern when he's the one fucking us over? Here I was worried that I'd have to beat his ass for the money, and he's worried about the ECs.

"I figured that, but they are rilin' up the other brothers. Figured I'd see what you had to say on it. Blu's off. He doesn't want to talk to me much these days."

I want to slam my fist into his face. The way he says it all, I want to fucking rip his damn head off. I can't believe he has the fucking balls to stand in front of me and act like nothing has happened. Like he isn't a damn thief.

"Shit is off, Chop. Things will come to light later. You know," I say bringing my cigarette to my lips and lighting it before I continue, "if there was somethin' happenin' inside these walls, it's best to fess up to it."

He watches me intently but doesn't say a word. It's like his mind is trying to decide on saying it or waiting it out. His eyes flicker with a slight fear, his body tensing up. For his sake, I hope he says it, but he doesn't.

"Well, fuck. I'll see you later. I'm gonna go see what Cherry's flashin' over there."

Chop grins, shaking off all the tension and walks away quickly when I hear the shots being fired. I stand up a little straighter when I hear

Mayhem screaming like a fucking madman, firing his gun into the air.

"Crazy son of a bitch," I mumble before heading inside. I need some vodka or Jack to get through this night.

Chapter 7

Brooke

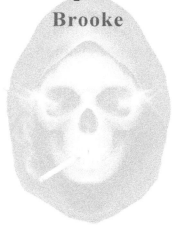

I yawn as I jog down the road. I got up entirely too early and couldn't fall back asleep. My thoughts keep drifting back to that night. If he would have asked me to fuck him instead of that gun, I would have done it. Is it sad that's it been that long? It's not that I don't have an interest in men. I do. It's just the kind of man that I want doesn't exist. Aside from the fact that I spend a majority of my time locked in a female strip club, I have no life.

I jog faster, push myself harder. Something in my life is going to have to give. I don't know what or how, but I need to actually get a life. Living vicariously through Angel isn't going to be an option anymore. She's moving on with her life.

She's going to college. She wants more out of her life than I do.

I make it to the gym in record time ready to get in the ring. I want to punch someone. I want to throw as many blows as I can. I want to fuck someone's world up the way mine is.

"You're here early," Charles, the owner, says when I walk in. I'm out of breath from pushing myself, but I'm ready.

I nod once before I say, "I know. Needed to expel this fucking energy somehow." He laughs, knowing me about as well as my own uncle.

I used to come here a lot with my dad. He trained here. Being a sheriff wasn't an easy thing to do, but he did it. Right up until that bastard shot and killed him.He started bringing me here when I was little, maybe three. I would watch him spar and I quickly fell in love with it.

"Tawny is here today. She'll spar with you." My heart kicks up a notch when he says that.

"Nice! I've been waiting to spar with her," I call out over my shoulder. I head into the locker room to get changed when I see Tawny. She's been a fighter as long as I have. We have that in common, she and I. We both need the release and we love it.

"Hey," she says when she notices it's me.

"Haven't seen you in a while," I tell her, pulling my shirt over my head.

I am grabbing my gear out of the locker when she replies, "I've been out of town. I don't know if you heard, but Rusty died."

My heart beats faster. Rusty was her brother and a damn good man.

"I'm so sorry. No one said anything to me. What happened?" I ask. Tawny and I always got along. Her dad is a cop like mine was. We basically grew up together.

"He got a call out in Vegas. MC war. He got in the middle of it and didn't come back out." She drops her head when she speaks. I walk over and pull her into a hug, knowing how hard it is to lose someone.

"I wish I'd known. I'm so sorry, Tawny," I whisper in her ear, knowing it won't make a bit of difference.

"It's life, right? Are you sparring with me today? I need to get out some energy, and Sherry won't do the trick." I laugh as I pull away from her and nod.

"Hell, she's like using a stand-up bag. She doesn't even fight back."

We both laugh before heading back out into the gym. We climb in the ring when Charles calls it. As soon as he tells us to go, we go. Tawny's body twists and turns as she dodges my punches. I go in full force. I need this as much as she does.

My fists fly at her before I throw in a kick landing in her ribs. That doesn't stop her, though. That's what I like about her; she won't give into me easily. That's what I need right now - someone who won't back down.

We spar for about forty-five minutes, draining ourselves. After we finish our session, I climb out and head toward the locker room.

"That was amazing. Teach me!" a little blonde squeals next to me. I turn my head to look at her, her eyes gazing into mine.

"I'm not an instructor. Sorry." I grab my towel and throw it around my neck when I notice her following me.

"I don't care. This isn't my usual hangout either, but here I am. Hey, you want to hang out later? There's a party if you want to come. I'm Cherry."

I look back over at her. She seems nice enough, although judging by the way she's dressed in a little short tight jeans skirt and tank top that shows off her skin, she doesn't belong around here. Her rambling is a little annoying and the fact that she's out of place usually would intrigue me, but I'm too worn out from my session with Tawny to care today.

"I don't really do parties, Cherry. If you want to come in on Saturdays, I'm usually here." She smiles before she licks her lips.

"Ok, the truth is this. I was asked by a friend to follow you around. He wants to meet you," she confesses. My steps quickly halt.

I narrow my eyes before I ask, "What friend? You're following me? Do you realize that this is where the local cops come to work out?" As soon as the words leave my mouth, Cherry's face falls. Her eyes widen. Yeah, didn't see that one coming, did she!

"Are you fucking kidding me? I will fucking kill Reggie and Mouse. Those little bastards!" she roars with the fury of a lion while stomping her foot. It's almost adorable on her little face until the last name she said hits me.

"Mouse?" I ask.

"Yeah, Mouse. That fucker. He said he saw you the other night but didn't get to talk to you," she rambles.

"I changed my mind. I'll go party with you." If Declan didn't want me to show up at his clubhouse and Mouse does, why not go? The chance to see Declan again is outweighing the rage he might feel when he sees me walk in those gates.

Her eyes light up before she asks, "Are you into girls?" I shake my head before she shrugs. "Could have been fun to fuck with them."

A small smile pulls across my face. I can like girls for tonight, though. Who the hell am I turn to turn her down? I'm always up for a dare or a good prank.

"Let's do that."

Chapter 8

Declan

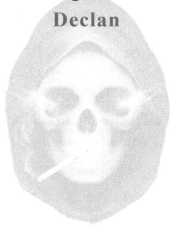

I pull the gun from my jeans and point it at the asshole. "You know how much I can't stand a liar?" He shakes his head, but he holds a strength in him that reminds me a lot of myself.

"Fuck you, Declan. I don't care what you think about me," he spits back. He should care. He should care deeply what I think of him since he wants to be a prospect for the Soulless Bastards.

"We don't let just anyone in here." I push the gun closer to his head. This is all a game. It's a scare tactic to see which one is worth our fucking time. If they cower in fear, they don't step foot anywhere near this clubhouse again.

"Say it again, boy," I growl. Nuts. That's the name I'm giving him if he says it again.

"Fuck you!" he says, blood dripping down his chin. Yeah, I may have fucked him up a little more than the others, but shit, he was the one testing my patience.

"Stand up, boy." I nudge him with the barrel of my gun. The kid hops up and stands in front of me when I wave Blu over.

"Looks like Nuts here needs a patch, brother," I say. Blu runs his eyes over the mess I made of the kid's face before he crosses his arms, glaring at him.

"You think you have what it takes to handle this life?" Blu asks. He watches the kid for a reaction. This isn't much different than the shit we used to go through. I may be a little tougher on them now than they were on me. I wasn't just a prospect, though. I was blood; I was born into this. Of course, I had to prove I was good enough. Maybe more than the others.

Nuts stands there stoically before he says, "I know I do." Blu nods his head before giving me that final glance. He gets the nod he wanted from me.

"Alright then. Nuts it is. Get one of the club girls to sew you a patch on that cut. You're the fuckin' runt. Don't forget it. A patched member tells you to fuckin' jump, you damn well better ask how high." The kid stiffens his back and nods when Blu passes him the prospect cut.

"The rest of you, you ain't shit. You won't ever be shit. Get the fuck up and drag your sorry asses outta my clubhouse!" As soon as the words leave Blu's lips, the boys are on their feet.

"Way to get 'em, Blu." Cherry's voice echoes through the room. I don't turn to look at her, but Blu does.

"Thanks, Cherry Bear. You got a new girlfriend?" Blu asks.

That catches my attention. I turn and see her. My jaw clenches. What the hell is she doing here? I told her not to come back.

"Yeah. Mouse and Reggie sent me to find her, but I thought about keeping her for myself," Cherry says, running her finger along Brooke's neck. Brooke doesn't make eye contact, but she smiles nonetheless.

"She looks like she's your speed. I'm Blu," he says, stepping toward her with his hand out. She steps up and takes it. "Brooke."

Blu's eyes linger on her a little longer than they need to.

"Watch out for these guys. They don't play by the rules, and I sure as hell won't make them," he warns her.

She nods her head once before stepping back next to Cherry. Where the hell did Cherry pick her up at? What the hell is she doing bringing her back here?

Blu turns on his heel and walks away when Cherry says, "Hey, Dec. You seen Mouse? I want to show off my toy." She wraps her arm around Brooke's body. I don't know what the fuck to say, so I stand there like a goddamn fool. She's with Cherry, of all fucking people.

"Should be cleanin' shit up and settin' up for the party. Why don't you go find him?" I suggest. Cherry starts to move, taking Brooke with her. Oh, like fuck she is!

"Leave this one." I put my hand up as Brooke tries to walk past, coming to rest on her stomach, stopping her from going anywhere. Yeah, I'm going to be that kind of asshole.

"She's mine, Declan," Cherry tries to protest. She better watch who the fuck she's talking to like that.

"This your clubhouse, Cherry?" I ask her, my anger rising higher and higher.

She doesn't look up at me, but I snap, "You better learn your place, Cherry. You been here a long time to act like you don't know the fuckin' rules."

She nods her head slowly before looking up at me, "Sorry, Declan." I nod once as her eyes slide to Brooke's. "Sorry, Brooke. I'll find the guys and come right back." Cherry turns on her heel and walks away.

"What the hell are you being a dick to her for?" Brooke's dark eyes quickly meet mine. Look at that. She has a whole lot of balls for a little thing.

I raise my hand and run my fingers over the butterfly that hangs from her neck. "I'm not being a dick. She knows the rules around here, butterfly. What are you doin' here? I thought I told you never to come back here." It wasn't much of a question, more of a statement. She doesn't belong here. My tone is daring. I'm daring her to respond to me. To tell me why she really came here and I have a feeling it wasn't for Cherry. No, she wanted to see me.

"She stopped by to see me and invited me to a party. I came. It was that was simple." She moves to take a step back, but I don't let her. I invade her space. My fingers drift around from the necklace to the back of her neck, pulling her face close to mine.

"You stepped foot into my clubhouse, my world. Do you have any idea what I could do to you?" I ask in a loud whisper. Her breathing has kicked up, and her heart is beating wildly. I can practically feel it.

"I didn't come here for you, so I'm going with nothing."

"They won't speak to you if I say the words." Her eyes burn with a fire that I want. I don't know if she wants to punch me or fuck me on the spot, but goddamn that tension is there.

"Will you say the words though, Declan?" Holy fuck! The way she says my name. I want to take her against this wall and show her who the fucking boss is around here but not now.

No, I'll save that for later.

Chapter 9

Brooke

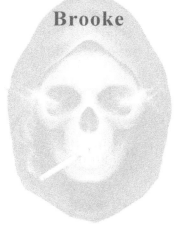

His mouth is inches from mine, his breath mingling with mine. The only thought I have is of him fucking me with that gun again. There was something so damn erotic about it. The cold steel sliding inside of me as I clenched around it. It was hot, sexy, and so fucking thrilling.

"What's wrong? Afraid of me?" he asks.

Fuck no! I'm not afraid of him. Turned on? Hell yes, but not afraid. The one thing I've learned growing up was not to be afraid of anything and if for some reason I was afraid, to never show that fear. My father instilled that in me, and it's always stuck. I raise my hand and rest it on his chest. Mistake number one on my part. The heat is pouring off him.

"I don't get scared. There is nothing in this place that I'm afraid of. You may hold some kind of power inside these walls, but that's as far as it goes." I see the look in his eyes. I'm pushing his buttons, pushing his whole belief system.

A growl tears from his throat. "You may want to rethink that. I own this town and everyone in it.

I smile and say, "Except me." I lower my hand when I hear Cherry's voice coming back toward us.

And here I was thinking this was going to be boring. I'm actually starting to enjoy this party.

"Found them!" Cherry says walking over to me.

Declan hasn't moved. I take a step around him and see the guys from the gate the other night.

"Hey," I say cheerily with a smile plastered across my face. I might as well piss Declan off a little more.

"Hey, sweetheart. Sorry we didn't get a chance to meet the other night. I'm Mouse." His hand comes out, but Declan quickly steps in between.

"She's off limits, Prospect." My eyes jump to his. Cherry huffs next to me. Declan looks down at us before he says smugly, "Look at that, butterfly. I accepted that little challenge." He moves to walk away, but I follow behind him. Who the hell does he think he is?

"You can't just do that! They have mouths, you know?" I stomp like a little girl trying to get her own way. It would be amusing if I wasn't so irritated. Here I was thinking I might just get a good one-night fuck and he's ruining it for me.

"They won't use them if they want to stay Prospects," he says, never turning to look at me. I don't stop either. Not when he turns down another hallway, not when he stops to sign off on papers being thrust at him.

"What the hell is with you? Why do you think you're the fucking ruler of the world?" I yell. He chuckles but keeps walking. I don't pay attention to where we're going. I just stomp along.

"I am the fucking ruler of the world," he says as he keeps going, still not looking at me.

He walks into a room, and I follow behind like the idiot that I am.

"You're really conceited, aren't you? Do you think the world revolves around you?

Everything needs to fall at your feet?" I stand here with my hands on my hips when I realize where we are. Well shit!

We appear to be in his room. Or someone's room. Declan steps around me, closing the door. Any other girl would freak out right now, but I'm a fighter - I can take him.

"The only reason you'd fall to your feet is to suck my dick. If that's your plan, let's get to it. If not, get out and send Cherry in." His words are like a slap in the face.

"You're a pig," I say, not moving.

"You're still here." He inches closer to me.

"You aren't even on my level." I glance at him, running my eyes up and down his body. I know it's a hard body. I've seen the way his shirt hugs every muscled inch of him.

"Is that a bet, butterfly?" he asks, his tone gravely and sexy as hell.

"Are you making it one?" I retort.

"I bet that by the end of the night, I have you naked."

Jesus, the way he says it makes me want to strip right now.

"Bet's on, big boy." Declan smiles, taking a step back.

"This is gonna be the best torture," he says, licking his lips.

"It is. You're going to be dropping at my feet before I ever slip my shirt off," I say before heading back out. I hurriedly make my way back outside to the party.

Chapter 10

Declan

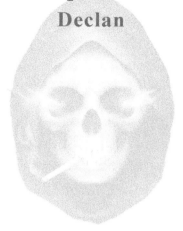

I should kill Cherry on the spot. How the hell does she, of all fucking people, find Brooke and bring her here? Better yet, how the fuck is she rubbing all up on her and Brooke is letting her?!

My balls ache after our encounter in my room. I wanted to take her by force right then and there, but she isn't one of our club whores.

"Who the hell is that?" Mayhem asks, tossing his arm over my shoulder.

"That's my challenge for the night." He chuckles before walking away. I watch as Cherry and Brooke dance together. The way Cherry grinds against her. Brooke isn't innocent in the movements either. Her hands run all over Cherry's body, tugging her in as closely as she can get her.

Her hips sway, pressing against Cherry in the most sexual way. Jesus Christ, this is going to get out of hand quickly. I see the way the other guys are eyeing her like she's a fresh piece of meat. Cherry knows what she's doing, too. Her lips skate down Brooke's neck. Brooke's mouth parts in response.

And yep, my goddamn dick is making a tent out of my jeans. I readjust it as I watch the scene unfold in front of me. I still can't believe that she's here.

I warned her away, but after the look I saw on her face after I fucked her with my gun, I knew she was trouble. My kind of trouble.

"Goddamn, leave it to Cherry to find the hottest lesbians around," Tic says. I glance over and nod my head.

"She won't be eatin' that tonight, though. I will," I say. Tic chuckles before slapping my shoulder.

"You may want to get over there then, 'cause Nick is movin' in for the kill. You know those girls fall at his feet lookin' like a pretty boy."

I turn my head to catch the brother Tic mentioned moving in. I let Nick take his chance because I know he won't get far. Brooke will shoot him down in a heartbeat. I watch the scene unfold

48

in front of me. Nick moves up in front of Brooke, pushing Cherry to the side. His hands land on Brooke's waist.

"Oh, look at that." Tic laughs when Brooke shoves him off. Her lips move to Cherry's neck before locking her gaze with mine across the yard.

"Fuck me," Tic growls at the scene. I know that feeling!

Her eyes stay connected with mine, playing her game. I can do one better. As I saunter over, her eyes never leave me. I move in behind Cherry, grabbing her ass in one hand. She squeals before looking over her shoulder at me. I get that cute little grin of hers before my hand slides around front slipping under the front of her skirt. Pushing her panties to the side, I slide my fingers through her wetness. She moans when Brooke pulls back to see what's happening. She takes in what I'm doing to Cherry before snapping her eyes back to mine.

"Tell me to stop and I will," I say more for the benefit of Brooke than Cherry. Her eyes dance between mine and the now closed ones of Cherry. Cherry moans, clearly enjoying what I'm doing to her. It doesn't matter that everyone is watching. It doesn't matter that there is a party going on. I do what I want when I want.

I work Cherry's clit a little faster and watch the way Brooke brings her lips between her teeth. She's trying to control herself right now, but it's too late. Cherry cums all over my fingers, which is no surprise, but what happens next sure the fuck is.

I slide my fingers out of Cherry slowly. Brooke's eyes are heated when she reaches for my hand. She brings my fingers to her mouth, her eyes on fire as she sucks the juice off. Cherry watches the scene unfold with a smile on her face, letting her orgasm slow. Brooke licks my fingers the way she would my dick. I can't help it; I give the fuck up on the bet. I lost and I don't give a shit.

"What is it you want?" I ask her. She slowly releases my fingers and lets her arms fall to her sides. I see Cherry walk away out of the corner of my eye, clearly done with our interaction.

"One night. One round of hot fucking sex."

I stand there with my eyebrows raised. Is she serious? "You're not shittin' me?" I ask all the while thinking this has to be a joke. Girls don't just come around here looking for a quick fuck. At least girls like her don't. She shakes her head before she steps closer to me.

"I don't care which one of you guys it's with either. I just want it." Her voice holds a demand that my dick likes. She may not care which brother it's with, but I sure as hell do. No one will be getting that pussy but me.

I let out a growl when she says, "You lost the bet."

"I know, and I'm about to pay the fuck up." I grab her hand and drag her back toward the clubhouse doors when Mouse comes out.

"Fuckin' hell, Dec. Does everything I want have to go to you?" he snaps, looking from me to Brooke. What the fuck did he just say? I release Brooke's hand long enough to punch the little fuck in the mouth. He falls back against the wall before I grab her hand once more and drag her inside. I won't stop until I get her in my room.

Chapter 11

Brooke

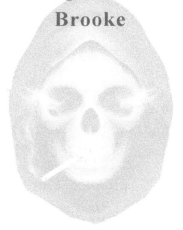

My body needs this. My mind needs this. I need the fucking release.

With all the drama at the club, I need a way to get out of my head for a while, and what better way than letting some hot man fuck it out of me. Declan slams the door before kicking his boots off. It's almost amusing to see how badly he wants this as much as I do.

"In a hurry?" I ask playfully when his darkened eyes meet mine. The heat building between us is consuming all the air in the room. He stalks toward me slowly, lifting my chin so that I'm looking at him when he reaches me.

"You sucked my fingers better than a lot of girls have sucked my dick. You teased me for hours out there with Cherry. Now you're gonna show me what the fuck this sexy little body can do," he growls the words, making my insides explode with heat.

I reach over and pull his shirt up and over his head, tossing it to the floor. His eyes follow my every movement as I slowly remove mine. Dec licks his lips as he stares at my chest. The way he's looking at them as if they are the best treat he's ever seen in his life. I know they are nice but damn.

"Fuck," He grumbles. I laugh when he looks up at smiles, "What? I'm a titty man."

I reach behind me and unclasp my bra, letting it slide down my arms. His eyes travel over the mounds on my chest before he leans down and takes my nipple with his lips. I moan at the feeling before he bites down. He quickly pulls back and grins.

"You like it rough, my little butterfly?"

I don't answer him; I'm too fucking turned on by his raspy voice to even try.

"Turn around," he growls. I do so slowly when I hear him breathe in sharply. His fingers travel over my skin, lighting it on fire.

"A whole back piece? I never saw that one comin'," he says softly as his fingers outline the large butterfly tattoo covering my entire back.

"Let me see if I can make you fly."

That's it. Those words were my undoing. I spin around, ripping at the buckle on his belt before shoving his jeans and boxers down his legs.

"Condom?" I snap my fingers at him. He's happy to give it to me. I rip the packet open and slide it on him quickly. His eyes never leave me. It's a little unsettling to have a man watching me this intensely. I've never been with a man like that before.

"How do you want me, butterfly?" he asks seductively.

"Balls deep inside of me."

He grabs my chin, holding it in place. Forcing my gaze to remain on his. His eyes practically glow with need.

"Just remember who asked for it," he says, leaning down and capturing my mouth with his. His kiss is hungry and not gentle in any way. In fact, I think he is trying to show me who the fucking boss is and in this moment, I'll gladly let him. He lifts me in his strong arms before breaking the kiss. Throwing me roughly onto the bed, he stalks over and yanks my shorts and panties down my legs before I can even think about anything else. As I lay here turned on by his actions, my shoes are torn off last and discarded to the floor.

He positions himself between my thighs, lifting my legs onto his shoulders. His eyes meet mine, and for a brief second, I think he's going to say something, but he doesn't. Without a word, he leans forward and sinks himself inside of me. I claw at his arms and scream his name. The deeper he gets, the more I realize how much I needed this. The stress of my everyday life, the lack of a sex life – all of it adding up.

His balls slap my ass with each and every thrust. The power behind him is astonishing. I've never had anyone fuck me the way Declan is fucking me right now.

As if he knew what I was thinking, he tells me, "Stop thinkin' about it. No one will be able to fuck you like me."

His words set me off. My pussy clenches around him, holding as tightly as it can.

"Goddamn!" he roars, his eyes closed in ecstasy, as I grin to myself.

"No one will ever fuck you like I can either," I reply saucily as I pump my hips.

His eyes pop open and lock on mine. We stare at each other as he plunges in deeper and deeper. My eyes slowly close again as I give into the pull of my orgasm. Just when I feel like I'm about to lose all control, he slows his movements.

"Open 'em! You will fuckin' watch me fill you," he growls. I snap my eyes back open and watch him. He pumps into me slowly until he realizes that he has my full attention. His hips take on a new speed. He thrusts harder and harder, his rhythm turning sporadic when I feel him swell inside of me.

"Fuck!" He roars just as he sends us both into a world where only pleasure exists. The high that I was chasing is now a reality, and I can't fucking get enough of it.

Chapter 12

Declan

My high has been blown for a week now. A week of club bullshit. A week of Chop's whining. A week since I fucked Brooke raw. I swear to you that girl's thighs were bruised and raw when she left here. I fucked her in ways that she will never forget. That was the point, wasn't it? She wanted a night of hot sex; she got just that and a little more. The problem now? I want her again. I want her on top of me. I want her riding me. I want her sweet pussy against my lips.

"How you been, Dec?" Griz asks as he struts into the room. He's a beast of a man I wouldn't want to mess with. I glance up from where I was picking at my beer label.

"I'm alright. Shit's just fucked, brother." He nods his head knowing exactly what he's doing here.

"I can imagine that. Shit's rough." Griz sits next to me, passing me a cigarette.

"I just don't get why he did it. It pisses me off. We're shorthanded as it is, man." I light the cigarette and blow out a ring of smoke.

"Heard that! I told Blu a few Nomads are lookin' to settle in somewhere. Might wanna see who's out there," he says.

I nod once. I already know all about that. Nomads are wanderers, though. So many times, I've heard of them trying to settle with one chapter or another, and they can't handle it. Staying in one place just isn't their thing.

"Butch still rollin' Nomad?" I ask, glancing over at Griz and see him nod in response.

"Past six years, brother. You would think that motherfucker would want a place to call home with his wife and all. Son of a bitch just keeps goin'." He chuckles.

"I suppose that works for some, yeah?" I ask.

Griz nods. Just then, we see Blu come out of his office, Kenderly not far behind him. She has a blush on her cheeks but still has that shy look. She looks up and tosses me a small smile.

Griz leans over and whispers in my ear, nodding toward Kenderly. "What's that about?"

"Fuck if I know, Griz. He's been watchin' her like she might run," I say.

He huffs. "Maybe she's tryin' to run. You know her daddy wouldn't want her here without him."

I nod again. That much I do know. Kenderly doesn't have any other family.

"You boys ready to handle the problem?" Blu asks, leaning against the bar in front of us. I look up into the dark eyes of my president, understanding he's about to do what no one ever wants to do to a brother.

"Fuck, I guess so," I grumble. I shove off my stool and round the bar, grabbing another beer.

"Where's he at?" I ask, glancing over at Blu. He drops his head before pulling it up and taking a breath.

"Out back. Let's get this shit over with, yeah?" Blu says before swallowing big gulps of vodka. I follow his lead and knock back a few myself. This shit is always harder than you think it will be.

He was family once. He was a brother, and now he's nothing but a traitor. Griz slaps a hand on Blu's back before we follow him down the hall and out the back door. The guys who rode down with Griz's chapter of Soulless Bastards stand amongst ours. It's a heartbreaking scene when you truly think about it. We're all family. Now that has to come to an end.

"Listen up!" Blu roars over the crowd. The yard goes silent, and all eyes fall to us.

"This club has rules. We follow those rules because it's what works. We make our own way of life, but we don't stray from the way things have always been. Times change. People change. The Brotherhood doesn't, though. So, when a brother decides to take matters into his own hands, it offends not only me but us as a club."

I can hear the murmurs go around. The looks. They want to know who it is.

Blu sucks in a breath before he starts again. "One of our brothers has been stealin' from us. Skimmin' money off our books. That's not tolerated." Blu's eyes find Chop's through the crowd. "Chop. You fucked up."

Like the fucking red sea, the guys part and leave him standing alone. He doesn't look upset or even nervous.

"You got anything to say?" I ask. Chop shakes his head.

"Line up!" Blu roars. "You are a coward. Get on your fuckin' knees," he growls at Chop.

He does what he is told; he drops to the ground on his knees facing his brothers.

The air is thick, but this is the way we handle things. That doesn't mean it makes it any easier.

"Ready?" Blu yells as all the men pull their guns, aiming them at Chop. My heart stutters in my chest for the briefest of seconds. Holding my gun aimed at my once-brother is harder than I thought it would be.

"We're brothers! We're family. We ride hard and fuck harder! We don't betray our family!" Blu roars before the word "Fire!" rings through the air.

In the matter of seconds, Chop's body is loaded with at least sixty bullets.

One of them being mine.

Chapter 12

Brooke

"Why are you telling me this right now?" I rest my head in my hands on the desk in front of me.

"Because I don't want to keep working with that shit," Savannah says. I pull my head up to look at her before I grin. Savannah is one of our dancers here.

"Let me get this straight. You want to be a stripper, but you don't want to take all your clothes off? Am I getting this right so far?" I almost laugh when the words come out of my mouth. What the hell did she think being a stripper was?

"Exactly! I knew you'd understand, Brookey." She smiles. I shake my head.

"No, don't get that fucked up, Savannah. I don't understand. You're a fucking stripper. You strip! What part of that is hard for you to understand?" I ask, getting annoyed with the whole situation. She's clearly a fucking airhead.

"Taking all my clothes off goes against my religion," she says. Ok, that's it. The laughter I tried to hold back has erupted. Her religion? I can't. I just can't today.

"Get out of my office," I say through the tears that fall down my cheeks. I don't think I've laughed this hard in a long time.

"So, I can leave my clothes on?" she asks dumbly. I double over, holding my stomach.

"No! You're a stripper. You have to strip, Savannah. If you don't want to, go find another job." I wave her off, not missing the huff that escapes her. I can't believe she even asked me that.

I wipe my eyes before shoving out of the chair and heading toward the back. I need to check inventory and reorder whatever was lacking. I'm happily counting boxes when I hear a noise behind me. If one of those dancers came back here, I swear to god she's fired.

"You might want to sneak back out of here before I see you," I yell through the room, turning back to the boxes in front of me.

"What if I don't?" a deep voice vibrates behind me.

I stand up slowly, straightening my back. I'm in the fighting mood. I'm ready for it. I crave it. I turn slowly and see the dark eyes of an unknown man standing in the back of my goddamn club.

"Who the hell are you?" I ask, crossing my arms over my chest.

He grins a dark, sinister smile. It should scare me, but it doesn't. I trail my eyes over his body, sizing him up. I've taken men his size before. He looks to be well built, but that won't stop me from giving it my all.

"I'm here to make a deal with your uncle," he says casually.

"And that deal would be?"

"Not involving you, little girl. I make deals with men, not little women." His smirk makes my hands clench.

"Well, my uncle isn't here. I am. I run this shit. What the fuck do you want?" I ask getting more pissed by the second. I look him over once more only to notice the leather vest he's wearing. Did Declan send him here? He wouldn't know about me working, here would he? No, he couldn't.

"I made Devon an offer a while back on behalf of my club. We want his answer." The man crosses his arms over his chest before he steps closer to me. I watch him intently, ready to make a move if he tries anything.

"The answer is no. Whatever the fuck it was, it's no." His nostrils flare, his smirk deepening.

"You're not in a position to tell me no." Before I can register what's happening, his fist collides with my eye. That bastard!

He throws another punch seeing as I didn't go down the first time, but I dodge it. My hands are up, ready for a fight. He comes at me again only to be on the receiving end of my fist. Blood sprays from his nose, and he stumbles back. He gives me a sinister smile as he licks the blood from his lip.

"You just signed your death warrant." He points at me. The fire in his eyes makes me smile. I don't know why I'm a sick bitch like that, but when a man thinks he's won, it gives me a power surge.

I step up to him, ready to throw down. "Bring it."

Someone clapping their hands pulls my attention. The big guy steps back quickly when the other comes into view.

"Impressive for a girl," the new man says. I look him over. He's a little bigger than this guy, but that doesn't mean shit.

"What is this, surprise visit day?" I snap.

He smiles a gorgeous smile. This one is actually pretty damn nice to look at. If he wasn't trying to steal my uncle's club, I might fuck him.

"Let me apologize for my boy here. He has no manners." He flicks his gaze to his bleeding friends before bringing those golden eyes back to mine. "Your uncle was in negotiations with us. He sort of skipped out on our meetin's. We just needed to see where his head was at."

"I don't know anything about that. You might want to show up when he's here," I tell him, reaching up to see if that other asshole split my eyebrow open.

The man in front of me brings his hand up. His thumb runs over the bruise that I'm sure is starting to form. He's gentle at first. It's strange, but then he presses his thumb into the swollen skin, causing me to cry out in pain.

"Tell your uncle that Craft is lookin' for him."

Chapter 13

Declan

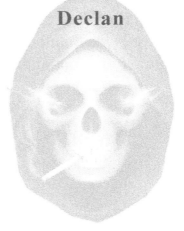

It's a somber feeling knowing that you put a bullet in the head of one of your brothers. That shit was almost a week ago. There's a strange feeling floating around the club. We all knew we had to do it, but that doesn't mean it hurts any less.

"You ready for that ride up to the northern chapter?" Blu slams his hand down on the bar in front of me.

I look up at him and nod. "Been ready. We need to get some new guys in here." Blu nods before grabbing a beer and popping the top off.

"Yeah, we got that member drive up there. Griz is pullin' a shit ton of weight around over there to get shit in order," Blu says, taking a long pull.

"Heard that. Rico was checkin' with the southern chapter. Said he had a few transfers." Blu nods in agreement.

We're all family. Regardless of what chapter you're in, we're family. We stick by family, and when one chapter falls short, they all make it a point to pull for the other.

"Yo, Declan! Got an issue out at the gate," Mouse yells through the front door. I shake my head with a grin on my face.

"Handle that shit and meet me in the office. I'm makin' a few calls," Blu says as he walks away from the bar.

I shove off my stool and head out the door when I hear screaming.

"What the hell?" I mumble under my breath. My boots hit the pavement a little harder when I hear it's a female voice. Please God, don't let one of those crazy bitches start shit today. Sometimes you kick a whore out and they just don't understand. They come back for more. I look over at Mouse, who has a smirk on his face. I want to punch the little fuck right now.

"Keep smirkin'," I point at him and say with a pissed off tone. That took care of that smile. Asshole.

"What the fuck is goin' on?" I ask Nuts as I step up to the gate.

"Dec, this crazy bitc-" he starts, but he doesn't get to finish. A fist flies, landing on his cheek. He stumbles back, slamming into the gate. I want to laugh, but goddamn, you can't come around here putting your hands on our prospects. I move around the gate ready for a fucking fight when her eyes find mine.

"Brooke? What the fuck happened to you?" I ask, noting the black eye she's sporting. A surge of anger rushes its way through me at the sight. My hands clench at my sides, ready to handle whatever she tells me. I don't know what the connection is I feel to her. Maybe I don't really feel it, I don't know.

"You son of a bitch! How did you know where I work? Huh? Why the fuck would you send your pigs after me?" she snaps, coming straight toward me. Her fist slams into my cheek before I can stop her. I'm stunned for a second, but quickly snap out of it. I wrap my arms around her body, pinning her arms in between her chest and mine. I think I have her under control, but the crazy bitch head butts me!

"You better calm the fuck down!" I roar, having had just about enough of her attitude. She fights me, but I adjust her and hold her tighter. Turning on my heel, I lift her squirming body held captive against mine and walk toward the clubhouse with a screaming Brooke in my arms.

"You son of a bitch! You had no right to do that!" she screams, but I have no idea what the fuck she's talking about. She's too irate to even talk to sanely right now.

"Calm down!" I growl.

"Fuck you. When you let me go, I'm going to fuck you up! All of you!" she roars. I just chuckle.

All the guys watch me as I carry this fighting little girl through the main room.

"Holy shit! Now that's my kind of girl!" Mayhem yells. I chuckle. I know she is his kind of woman. One that will fight him. I get to my room and head in, kicking the door closed behind me.

"I'm gonna put you down. Don't fight me," I warn her. Her body stills until I set her on her feet. Then it's an all-out war. She comes at me full force.

"I'll kill you!" she roars, her fist slamming into my chest. This is bullshit. I grab her around the waist roughly, jerking her against me. I walk toward the bed and toss her on before climbing on with her. Grabbing the rope off the nightstand, I wrap it around her wrists.

Yeah, I have fucking rope on my nightstands. You never know when you might need that shit. I'm always prepared!

Securing her to the bed, she screams and hollers, her legs flailing through the air. Fuck, she's a strong little shit! As I scoot down the bed, I catch a foot to the jaw. No way that's happening again. I grab her ankle and secure it to the bed too before doing the same to the other one.

"You need calm the fuck down. You got about one more time to kick me," I warn her. Her eyes narrow in on me.

"Or what? What the fuck are you going to do?" she hisses at me.

"Don't test me, darlin'," I warn her. She grins at me. She actually fucking grins at me.

"Fuck you, Declan. You better untie me." She grinds her teeth, looking sexy as fuck. Damn, I wish she was naked and tied to my bed.

"You better be calm when I come back," I say, pointing at her. I get off of the bed and I walk toward the door.

"You can't leave me in here!" she screams out even louder.

"Oh, babe. You walked up to my gates throwin' a little fit. I can do whatever the fuck I want."

Chapter 14

Brooke

This is great. This is just fucking great. I'm tied to that asshole's bed. The sad thing is? I like it! It was hot the way he threw me around. What kind of sick fuck does that make me?

I try to pull at the ropes.

"Oh, he's good," I mumble under my breath. Typically, I would be able to get out this, but he must tie things up a lot. He has skills, I'll give him that. I hear footsteps and wonder if that's the asshole coming to untie me, but when the door opens, it's not him.

"Jesus Christ! I knew that motherfucker was a freak." The man standing there is just as big as Declan. He's hot, too. His long blonde hair hangs around his shoulders, his perfectly straight teeth gleaming as he smiles. Yep, he's fuckable.

"Untie me, please," I say smoothly, trying to play him. His eyes roam over my body, but he doesn't move.

"You want me to lose a limb? My VP would kill me for even bein' in here right now," he says but doesn't make a move to leave.

"What's your name?" I ask.

"They call me Mayhem." He grins like he's proud of that. He probably is.

"Could you just untie me, Mayhem? I want to leave." He walks closer to the bed, my heart kicking up a notch. He reaches down and runs his fingers over my leg.

"You're the one Declan had the other night, huh?" he says dragging his fingers up my thigh.

"Maybe," I say softly. He reaches my mound and stops. His fingers are so close to me that I can feel the burn.

"He seemed to enjoy you. Wonder if you taste as good as I think you do." The way his eyes darken when he looks at me makes me shiver. It's scary in a way.

"I don't. Please, just untie me." I tug at the ropes again. I notice that every time I fight, the bulge in his jeans gets bigger. Sick fuck.

"He won't do that."

That voice. It sends my body into overdrive. That deep sexy fucking rumble. Why the hell does a man's voice hold that much power over a woman?

"You playin' nicely with my girl, Mayhem?" Declan asks as he walks around the end of the bed. He looks at me before dragging his eyes to his friends.

"Yeah, I was wonderin' what she tastes like. Those lips are utterly fuckable." Mayhem licks his lips while he looks at me.

"Don't let me stop you from gettin' a taste."

My heart tumbles in my chest. I jerk my eyes to meet Declan's. He has this evil smirk on his face that I want to slap the fuck off him, but at the same time, I want his lips on me, not his friend's.

Mayhem growls deep in his throat before leaning down closely. His breath skates over my skin the closer he gets to my lips. He holds his position, staring down at me.

"I dunno if I should let her taste me, though," he says against my lips.

My breathing catches in my throat. Do I want him to kiss me? No, I want Declan to kiss me. I want that feeling that only he can give me. The way my heart stuttered when he took me. The way he bruised my thighs with his hips.

"Meet me outside," Declan growls. Mayhem groans but he moves away from me.

I hear the door click as I look back over at Declan.

"You calm your ass down now?" he asks, his large arms crossed over his chest.

"Why would you send someone after me? I didn't do anything to you," I say softly. His eyes burn through me. Straight to my fucking soul.

"I assume that *someone* did that to your face?" he asks, nodding toward my eye. I turn my head away from him. I feel the bed shift before his large warm hand cups my cheek.

"I didn't send anyone after you, Brooke. I dunno what the fuck is goin' on with you."

I turn my head, and I can tell by the look in his eyes that he's telling me the truth.

"You didn't send any guys to the club?" I ask, confused by all of this. Dec shakes his head before reaching up and untying my arms. I sit up and watch as he does the same with my ankles.

"Who hit you?" he asks as he pulls the last of the rope free. Suddenly feeling vulnerable, I pull my knees up to my chest. I don't like this feeling.

"Doesn't matter. I need to go." I uncurl myself and shove off the bed, but he's there before I can take two steps. His hand comes up, wrapping around the back of my neck.

"You punched one of my prospects. You fuckin' kicked me, and you think you're just walkin' out of here?" he asks.

My heart slams in my chest. I can fight. I know I can, but Declan is much bigger than I am. The prospect wasn't that big!

Fuck. I'm fucked.

Chapter 15

Declan

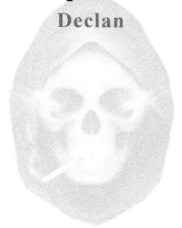

She isn't scared. That's not the look in her eyes. It's something else, but I can't place it.

"I'm sorry I hit you guys," she mumbles a fake apology. It's cute coming from her.

"Fuck that. You gonna tell me who hit you?" I growl. That's what's pissing me off the most. I want to know what idiot had the balls to put his hands on her.

"No one." She raises her head in a defiant posture. Look at her! She's testing my fucking patience and all I can think about is getting her naked beneath me. What is it about this woman?

"That's how you want to play this?" I ask her to give her a chance to rethink it. She doesn't move or say a word.

I lean down, my lips close to hers. "Last chance." She still doesn't move. Fuck, she is stubborn, and it makes my dick hard. I move closer, letting my lips linger on hers. She moans, slipping her tongue into my mouth. Goddamn, this woman is going to kill me.

I back her up until her legs hit the bed and she sprawls on the bed. Then she's fair game. I lean over and yank her jeans down her legs with her panties. Her pussy is gleaming, ready to be taken. I grin when I run my fingers through her wetness. She's fucking soaked.

"You wanted me that whole time, didn't you? You like bein' tied to my bed?" I ask her but not really giving a shit what she says. I can see how fucking wet she is and how hot her body feels. She's fucking craving my dick right now. I lean down and kiss her stomach. Brooke arches her back pushing her flesh into me. I growl and nibble at her skin.

"Tell me, baby," I say as I slide down, positioning myself between her legs. Brooke pushes up on her elbows, watching me. Fucking Christ this girl is wild, and I fucking love it.

"You wanna watch me eat this pussy?" I ask as I blow gently on her wet body. She arches her back and gasps. I slowly lick one long pass over her. Her eyes widen, but I just grin. I lean back in and lick her like she's a fucking lollipop. I dip my tongue inside of her and twirl it around, but the whole time our eyes stay locked on each other. Not breaking that connection, I run my fingers over her skin on her thighs. I drag it up slowly, sliding one inside of her. I work her over before slipping a second inside. Curving my fingers, I find her sweet spot before I suck harder on her clit. Brooke's mouth hangs open; she's panting, gasping for air.

"Who hit you, baby? Tell me, and I'll make you come." She shakes her head no. I bring her closer and closer, but until she gives me what I want, I'm not giving her what she wants. I slow my pace, leaving her clit to the cool air of the room.

"Dec!" Brooke cries out my name. It's such a fuckin' sweet sound, too.

"Tell me, Brooke. That's all you have to do." I lean down and slowly take another long lick. "Say who it was and I'll let you come." My fingers keep moving as she presses her body into me. She wants this; I know she does.

"I don't know! I don't know who they were! They were bikers. They had vests like yours!" she cries out.

I lean my head back down, sucking and licking. My fingers are fucking her at the same pace my dick would if I were inside of her.

"Dec! Oh, fuck!" She screams just as her orgasm washes over her. Clenching around my fingers, she holds them hostage.

Her juices flow, but I lick every last drop from her. She tastes like perfection, and I want every drop of it. I ease my fingers out of her slowly noting the groan that escapes as I do.

"You taste perfect," I tell her. Her face is flushed, little beads of sweat dripping down her temples. Fuck! She's beautiful.

"You said you don't know who they were?" I ask her again. She shakes her head, trying to catch her breath.

"Besides the cut, did you notice any other patches or anything on them?" She turns her head to look at me.

"Cut?" she asks.

"The vest he was wearin'. It's called a cut." She nods slowly before she sighs.

"No. I didn't really see anything else. I was kind of busy," she says as she points at her eye. I lean in and brush my lips over the swollen flesh.

"I'll find out who hurt you," I whisper against her.

She jolts and leaps up. Frantically looking for her clothes, she grabs them when she sees them. I watch her tug her jeans back on quickly, stuffing her panties into her pocket in her haste to get away.

"I don't need you interfering in my life," she states.

My heart hammers in my chest. The way I feel like I need to protect her is overwhelming to say the least. Something about Brooke sets the beast inside of me off and all I want to do is make sure she's safe. Yet she can't seem to get that through her head, and it's infuriating.

"How many times are you gonna come to my clubhouse and think that I have no say in shit?"

Chapter 16

Brooke

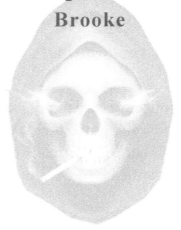

Oh, he is good. This fucker and his way of thinking are damn good.

"Who in the fuck do you think you are? I came here because I thought you had something to do with it!" I buckle my jeans and readjust my shirt.

"You came here so I'd fuck you," he retorts, as he stands there looking smugly at me.

"You think way too highly of yourself, Declan," I toss out as I turn on my heel. I head out the door, but I can hear him right behind me. I pick up my pace and slam right into a brick wall, or so I thought. I put my hands up and find a sweaty chest awaiting me. I drag my eyes up and find the same dick who was in the room earlier, Mayhem.

"If you wanted to touch me all you had to do was ask," he says with a smirk. I try to pull my hands away, but his larger ones capture my wrists, holding them in place.

"Believe me, I didn't want to," I mumble.

"You caught my butterfly." Declan's voice booms from behind me, a hint of laughter in his voice.

"She wanted to get her hands on me," Mayhem says, never pulling his eyes from mine. I roll my eyes and tug again. This time he lets me go.

"I bet she did," Declan says with a chuckle.

"I have never met any men who were so into themselves. You guys really think you're something special," I state with my hands on my hips.

"That's 'cause we are special." I hear another voice. Jesus Christ.

I look to my left to find another man, shirtless with sweat dripping down his chest. He's older than these two.

"Can I just leave?" I ask, looking between the three.

"Who the hell are you?" the other guy asks.

"This is Blu, our president. This is Brooke," Declan says. Blu eyes me up and down. I think I saw him the other night, but I can't be sure.

"Nice to meet you again. We met at the party," he says, being polite.

I nod once and say, "Yeah, you too. Can I leave?" I ask him.

His eyes move from mine to Declan's before slowly slipping back to me again. "I don't know. Ask my VP. He seems to like you." Blu chuckles and walks away. I blow out an exasperated breath.

"Who is the goddamn VP!" I roar. The guys laugh when Declan places a hand on my shoulder.

"I am. Thought you knew that," he says, his breath closer to my ear.

"I'm never getting out of here." I blow out an exasperated breath. Declan laughs before throwing his arm over my shoulder.

"Come on, sweetheart. I'll walk you home," he says as he leads me through the hallways.

When we step outside, I take a deep breath and settle the nerves racing through me. I take in the yard that is now littered with cans and beer bottles.

"You guys are disgusting," I mumble as we head toward the gate.

"Yeah, things got a little out of control last night," Declan says, kicking a can across the yard.

When we step onto the sidewalk, I stop and look up at him. "You really didn't send anyone after me?"

Declan shakes his head before bringing his hand up to my cheek. "You do realize we aren't the only club around here, Brooke. There are more. If I knew the whole story, I could help you out." He seems so sincere and honest, but I don't trust him. Not with this.

"I don't need any help," I say. I turn and walk toward the house, but Declan isn't far behind me.

"Why are you so stubborn?" he asks. I glance over my shoulder and raise my eyebrows at him.

"Stubborn?"

"Yeah, stubborn. Don't you see I'm just tryin' to help you out?"

"Why, Declan? You don't know me. You don't know anything about me." He closes his eyes and stops walking, but I keep walking. It's true. I'm almost to my house when he speaks again.

"Maybe I want to."

I stop and turn to face him. I watch the way his jaw tics, the vein in his neck throbbing.

"No, you don't. You like the idea that I'm different than Cherry. I'm not naive, Declan. It's the same reason I-" I stop myself from saying what I really want to say. I want to tell him that that is the reason I like him too. That he's different from all the other guys. That he's like no one I've ever met, but I don't know him any more than he knows me.

"The same reason you what?" he asks, crossing his arms over his chest.

"Nothing. I need to go. I'm sorry I accused you. It was a fuck up on my part." I turn to head across the street when Declan stops me again. His voice sends a shiver up my spine.

"You know where I am, Brooke. If you need anything, don't hesitate to come down."

I drop my head slightly. I don't want to rely on a man. I don't need his help.

At least that's what I keep telling myself.

Chapter 17

Declan

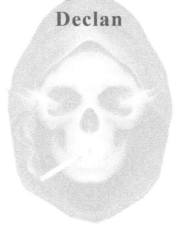

"What are you doin' here?" I ask when Brooke is standing at the front door of the clubhouse. Mouse must have let her come up.

"I was…I don't know what I'm doing here." She looks down at her hands, clearly not the girl that I met. She's closed off, in her own head. I know what she needs. I know what she wants. I reach for her and lift her chin, her eyes coming to lock with mine.

"You want me?" I ask her calmly. I think she needs it. I think she needs me. She needs that release, and I always give it to her.

"You are so conceited," she says, shaking her head. I grin like a fool. I know what I can do for her. I know what I have to offer.

"Come on," I tell her. Brooke walks in but doesn't look at anyone. I don't care either. I walk her straight into my room, kicking the door shut behind me.

"You wanna tell me what's wrong with you?" Brooke shakes her head, reaching for the hem of her shirt. My eyes follow her movements. Taking her in. She's fucking gorgeous, and I want every drop of her.

"In a hurry, butterfly?" I ask as I slip my cut down my arms and quickly yank of my shirt. She watches me, setting my body on fire. The lust races through my veins.

"I need it, Dec," she says softly.

I know she does, and I'm the one to give it to her. Toeing my boots off, I pull my jeans down my legs, kick them and my boxers to the side, and stalk toward her.

"You want it hard, butterfly?" I ask her.

She gazes up at me with a fire burning in her eyes. She looks so fucking perfect. Her beautiful round tits with the nipples hardened. I want to suck them into my mouth and never let them go.

"Fuck me, Declan. That's what I want," she nearly growls at me.

I reach for her, jerking her into my chest. I watch the way her breathing comes faster the closer she is to me. I study her face. I study her eyes. The way they hold my gaze, never breaking away. She's beyond anything I thought I'd find around here. She is the opposite of what I'd ever wanted, but at the same time, I see more inside of her that I want to get my hands on.

I slide my hands down her back, gripping her ass roughly. The gasp that falls from her lips makes my dick harden even more.

"I'm gonna fuck you, Brooke. That wasn't even up for debate. How I'm gonna fuck you is," I tell her. Her eyes widen as she sucks in a breath. There it is. I got her where I want her.

I lean my head down, sucking the flesh of her neck into my mouth. She moans, and that's about all of that I can handle. Her reactions drive me insane. Lifting Brooke in my arms I walked us to the bed, laying her down gently.

She watches me the whole time I rip the condom open and slide it on. Her gaze is burning so deeply into me that I can barely calm the feelings racing through my body. I need inside of her. All that consumes my mind is the idea of fucking owning her. I lift her leg, hiking it around my hip.

"I'm gonna take you hard," I warn her before slamming inside of her. I get so deep that I choke up. Brooke's pussy clenches, and I swear to God, I won't be able to hold out long. I know how bad she needs this, but fucking help me, I need it more.

Chapter 18

Brooke

Declan holds my arms above my head with one of his hands. My mind is whirling with every thrust of his powerful hips. He's lost in the sensations flowing between us. I raise my hips trying to pull him in deeper. I need this. I need the release. I need to feel. Declan must know what I need. He can sense it. He doesn't ask, he just gives, and I think that's what keeps calling me back to him.

He plunges into me, and my body reacts. My pussy locks down of its own accord, trying to keep him inside of me. That's the only place I want him. I want him to own me. I want him to pound into me so roughly that I will feel him for days, needing to feel the pain paired with the pleasure that he inflicts has me writhing beneath him.

"You like that? You like when I hurt you?" He asks, looking down at me breathlessly. His eyes glisten in the light of the room. The way he watches me, I almost come undone.

"Harder." The only word that will form on my lips makes him smile.

Declan grins before pulling out of me slowly. Just as I'm about to protest, he slams back into me roughly. My body jerks and spasms as he takes me harder, just like I asked him to.

"Yes!" I cry out as the warmth floods me. My stomach tingles, my heart beats rapidly. I want this more than I have anything else in a long time - to feel him explode inside of me, to feel the weight of him on top of me. It's all my mind can do to focus on the moment at hand.

"Brooke!" Declan growls my name. I pry my eyes open and look up at him. His movements slow, his hand moving between my legs.

He rolls his hips, touching me so deeply. His thumb circles my clit and lights flash behind my eyes. My orgasm takes me by surprise. I come harder than I ever have before with Dec right behind me. My pussy clenches, milking Declan for everything he has. His face is contorted in pleasure as his release takes him over the edge. He grunts and groans as I feel his dick twitching inside of me. He releases my hands, and I instantly bring them to his shoulders, holding him tightly.

"Was that hard enough for you?" He smiles down at me.

"That was perfect."

Chapter 19

Declan

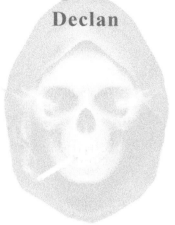

The last few weeks have consisted of business meeting after business meeting. It's almost annoying as fuck, but it has to be done. Brooke has been around to get fucked more times than I can count. I'm not complaining. She's growing on me.

The club has signed off on new shipments of guns from our overseas provider and business is running smoothly. Aside from our lack of manpower, this club is kicking ass. Soulless Bastards have always been on top. The more we push ourselves, the more we work. We know how to run business. We know how to take care of it, too. Since Chop's been gone, we have seen the money start to stack up. We knew where it was going but having it back where it belongs is nice.

"Why are we even doin' this? We have strippers at the clubhouse," I grumble as we walk into Leggs, a fucking strip club.

"Shut the fuck up. Maverick wanted his party here," Blu says. I just groan. We have fucking strippers. If we don't, give me ten minutes and we'll get some. Wasting time and money coming here isn't my ideal solution.

I glance around, but there is nothing here I want. "Such a waste."

We pull up chairs and sit around the table when a pretty little thing walks up to us.

"What can I get you, boys?" she asks. I glance over, running my eyes up and down her body. She isn't bad looking, but working here, I'd guess that she's as used up as the club whores.

"Whiskey," I tell her.

She nods before going around the table taking orders. My eyes fall on the stage at the front when the lights dim and the music begins. Same old acts. The girl spins around the pole, does her thing. It used to get me hard watching them. Not anymore, though. It's always the same thing over and over. There are never any new moves, just the same shit on repeat.

"I'm goin' to piss," I tell Blu. He gives me a nod as I shove out of the chair. I stalk across the room when I see a woman with her hair piled up on her head. I let my eyes drag down her body taking in her knee-high heeled boots and sexy-as-sin ass in those tight-fitting jeans. I adjust my dick as I walk past her. But when she yells at the guy in front of her, I stop dead in my tracks. That voice. I turn around and look at her. She's telling this man off, and it's sexy as fuck.

I can't move. I stand there like a goddamn fool entranced by her little rant. The guy she's yelling at looks over at me, but I can't take my eyes off her. After a few seconds of him not paying attention she turns her head to see what the fuck he's looking at.

"Oh, for fuck's sake!" she yells. "What the hell are you doing here?" She moves toward me with the look of anger etched into her face. She's hot as fuck like that, too.

"What the fuck are you doin' here? You a stripper?" I ask her. I know she isn't. At least judging by what she's wearing I wouldn't guess her to be.

"Are you serious right now?" she asks, narrowing her eyes at me.

"You're in a strip club, butterfly." I motion around with my hand. She raises her eyebrows before she huffs.

"I have too much work to do to deal with you." She stomps past me, and God fucking help me, I follow behind her. I see her smile and nod at some guy who I assume is a bouncer before she walks down a back hallway. I try to follow her, but the man stops me.

"You can't go back there," he says. I look down at his hand on my chest before I lose it.

"Now you decide who can and can't go back there?" I ask, putting two and two together. This is the club she was talking about. This is where someone came after her. "Where the fuck were you when someone punched her in the fuckin' face?" I raise my voice.

"That won't happen again," the guy snaps at me.

"You know what, you're right. It won't, 'cause if it does, I will fuck your whole world up." His eyes widen before he steps up closer to me. That's when I hear her.

"Let him past, Nick," Brooke hollers down the hall. Nick turns to look at her, but I don't. I keep my eyes trained on this little fuck who let her get hurt. Nick steps back, but I don't move.

"She ever gets hit on your watch again, I'll come back for you," I say when only he can hear me.

Nick nods slowly before I turn and walk down the hall. Brooke walked into the last room, and that's where I head.

"What kind of security you got workin' here? I hope he's not all of it," I say, pointing toward the door. Brooke's eyes come up from the desk she was staring down at to meet mine.

"For now he is." She looks away quickly before I let out a growl.

This is bullshit.

Chapter 20

Brooke

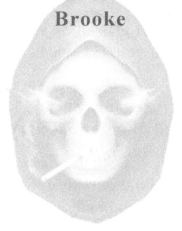

There's a deep rage simmering in those gray eyes. He's mad. I don't know why he cares, but I can see the look. I look back down at the paper in front of me, trying to avoid his gaze. It's harder than I thought it would be too.

"You know that's bullshit, right?" he says. I take a deep breath and look up at him.

"It is but when you have a fucking budget, you make it work," I say calmly. I've looked into a hundred different ways to try to get this club back up and running at full speed and security wasn't high on that list considering we haven't had any problems.

"One fuckin' bouncer? He doubles as security?" Declan's eyes blaze with fire.

"Yep, one per shift. That's all I can afford at the moment. One bouncer." That's all he's getting. The only thing he's doing right this minute is making my goddamn panties wet, and I don't like it. I don't like that he is affecting me. I don't like that I'm letting him.

"This your club?" he asks, his voice calming slightly as he runs his hand over his face.

"My uncle's club, but I run it most of the time."

"I didn't realize this place was still open," he says, dropping into the chair across the desk from me.

"It's barely open. That's why I'm here. My uncle can't handle it on his own. He asked me to come in and see what I could do with it so he wouldn't have to shut it down," I admit to him.

Declan nods his head before looking around, "I hope a remodel is on the list of things to do."

I huff out a breath before I smile. "A remodel is nowhere near the top of the list. Did you miss the part about having one bouncer?" He gives me a sad smile before scratching at his neck.

"Loan?"

"Maxed out."

"Fuck!" he says. I nod. Yep! My feelings exactly.

"I'm doing the best I can. Changed out beer distributors - that saved us a little. I'm still trying to look at it all, though. It's time consuming," I tell him.

"I bet it is. I got a few connections on the liquor end. Might get you a better rate than you are now."

I pull my eyes up to meet his.

"That would be great. Thanks." He nods and looks around the small office. He has more to say. I wait for it. Declan leans forward, resting his elbows on his knees before looking at me.

"How much would it take to get you in the green?" His eyes burn straight through me. My body comes alive when he's this close to me. I shake my head, trying to focus on his questions rather than my hormones.

"Doesn't matter. I'm nowhere near that," I tell him. It's true. I've played with numbers for over a week. This club was once a money machine.

"Previously, they rolled in at least a million a year. Recently, income has dropped by seventy-five percent, and with the amount we are putting out for all of the accommodations and paying the girls - we're going under. The liquor prices have gone up. The girls are demanding more and more money. Our DJ was offered a better paying job and has asked for a raise. You know the area has had a higher crime rate lately, which is driving out our upper-class businessmen."

"Not what I asked you," he says.

"To be back where we need to be and actually start making a profit, I guess somewhere in the upper hundred thousand area," I snap. I watch his face. That number didn't faze him even a little. Declan leans back in his seat, his thumb trailing so fucking sexually over his bottom lip. You can tell he's lost in thought. I wouldn't know what the fuck he's thinking though.

"I'll front it," he finally says.

I shake my head with a grin on my face.

"Not a chance in hell."

"Why the fuck not? You need bailed out; I see this as a great fuckin' investment," he says, shrugging his shoulders.

"I don't want your shit mixed up in this! Are you insane? I didn't ask you for a handout!" I snap. I've never asked for help. Not with something like this. I'm not stupid, and I can handle it myself. Bringing Declan and his guys into this will just make it that much worse.

"I'm not offerin' a handout. I'm offerin' a business deal," he says calmly.

"No," I say firmly.

"Why not?" He leans forward, watching me.

"I don't want your deal, Declan. Do I look stupid to you?" I glare at him.

"Not at all." He stares back at me.

I swallow hard before I stand up and walk around the desk. "I appreciate the offer, Declan. Like I said, you don't know me. This isn't my club to take offers on anyway, and if it were, the answer would still be no," I tell him as I pull the door open. Declan stands and moves toward me. He stops when he's next to the door.

"You are stubborn as hell, and you have no fuckin' idea how much I like that." He looks down at me with a grin on his face. "The offer stays open if you ever want to take it."

He leans down, brushing his lips against mine slowly. His kiss is soft and sweet. Not like the man I've come to know in him.

"I'll see you soon."

Chapter 21
Declan

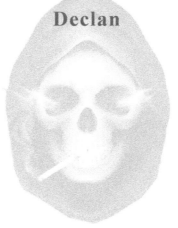

"Heat's comin' down on us," Blu says. I look up from the joint I was rolling.

"From where?" I ask.

"Not sure. I told Chandler to get a fuckin' handle on it or I'll turn his ass over to his captain myself," Blu says with a pissed off tone. I chuckle slightly.

"Hated that motherfucker since the day he started workin' for us," I tell him. Chandler is a cop we have on our payroll. I can't stand the little bastard, but he's never failed us before.

"They're hittin' everything around. It ain't just us. We need to ride out North anyway," he says. I nod once before lighting my joint.

"What was that shit at Leggs the other night?" he asks, leaning back in his seat.

"Brooke works there. Her uncle owns it."

"Didn't strike me as the type to own no damn strip club." Blu laughs at the thought.

"Fuck no! It's got a lot of promise and used to bring in big money. Said the fuckin' club is goin' under. I offered to help her out. She didn't want it," I tell him.

"She may take you up on it later. You should get her to ride with us."

I look at Blu when the words leave his mouth. I can't believe he, of all people, just said that to me. Blu doesn't like outsiders anywhere near our shit, let alone on a fuckin' ride to our sister chapters.

"What the fuck for?" I ask, inhaling.

"She makes you different. I like you when she's around - you ain't such an ass," he says on a laugh.

"Fuck you! She's been around a few times, Blu," I tell him flipping my hand through the air.

"Yeah, a few times you weren't such a dick." He laughs.

"She's got the club to handle." I shove out of my chair and head toward the door. "I'll be back later. Got some shit I wanna handle before we ride."

"Heard that."

I walk into the main room and see Tic standing against the bar looking rather pissed.

"Where's your head, brother?" He brings his eyes to mine.

"Gone. I just heard that Saints Crossing might cross the fuckin' line, man."

My eyes widen when he says that. Saints Crossing is another MC just on the outskirts of town. They've never been a problem for us before, but they've always wanted a little more reach than we were willing to give them.

"You talk to Blu?" I ask immediately. Tic shakes his head. "Just heard it. Was waitin' on you to come out."

"Get the fuck in there and tell him. I got some shit to handle. I'll be back soon." Tic nods before heading toward the office. This isn't what we need right now.

The last time we had an issue with Saints was when my dad was the fucking president of this club. He didn't handle things back then the way we do now. He was always on the fence about fighting over territory. Now? We will fight to the fucking death because that's what we do. This is our land. No one makes a move on it without us saying it's ok. It's a funny thing to think about for me. My father wouldn't fight for his land, but he would make his fifteen-year-old son kill a man in cold blood while his kids watched it happen.

I walk over to my bike and grab my helmet, my mind whirling with ideas. A straight fucking ambush sounds good to me right about now. I don't care who gets in the middle. We will take them all out. One by fucking one.

I rev up my bike and pull out onto the road, throttle it, and go. I need to feel that speed. I need to feel the rush I get when I ride, the way the bike rumbles beneath me. A lot of people call it a death machine, and if you don't know how to handle it properly, it could be. That's not me. I know how to handle my machine; I've been riding since I was a kid.

The first time my dad threw my ass on the back of his bike I was three. He thrust an oversized helmet into my hands and told me to hold the fuck on. I did, too. I loved it – everything about it. It sent a thrill through my body that nothing could compare to. I guess the asshole did one thing right with me.

I roll through town without a care in the world at the moment. Everything drifts away when I ride. Things will still be there when I get back, but for now, I'm free of it all. I'm about to take the next left through town when I see her standing on the sidewalk. I'd know that ass of hers anywhere.

I pull up at the curb and cut the bike off. I know she heard me pull up. The two other girls she's with are staring, but Brooke refuses to make eye contact with me. It stirs up something unusual in my chest.

"You tryin' to avoid me?" I ask. Brooke slowly turns to face me, a haunted look crossing her face.

I climb off the bike quickly and move toward her. Cupping her cheek in my hand, I bring her eyes to mine.

"Talk to me. What's goin' on?" I ask again.

Her eyes fill with tears before she says, "My uncle's dead."

Chapter 22

Brooke

My heart breaks in my chest. It's in pieces that will never be able to heal. I lost my dad and now my uncle. My family is slowly dwindling down to nothing. It's a hard reality to have to face. The cop that came to the house to tell me about his death was sincere. He said they would investigate it but nothing seemed out of the ordinary in his suicide note. One bullet to the temple. That's what they said. One of the girls apparently went to his house to hook up. It wasn't uncommon with him. They told me that she found him in the living room. The same living room we used to spend Christmas and holidays in.

"I'm not going," Angel says softly. I whip my head up and look at her.

"Oh, you are going! You are going to school, and that's not up for debate," I snap at her as tears trail down my cheeks.

While I spoke with Angel, Declan moved off to the side using his phone, but I can still feel his presence. Just having him near helps.

"I don't want to leave you, Brooke," she says, wiping at her own tears.

"I'll be fine. I'm a grown woman. I have the club to get in order." I don't know what else to say. She isn't putting her life on hold for me. That's not an option.

"She's right. I'm here, she's got me," Declan says, his hands landing on my shoulders. He stands behind me, his hard chest pressed into my back. He's quietly giving me strength. I'm thankful for it at the moment; I need it.

"I really don't want to leave you, Brooke," Angel cries again before throwing her arms around my neck.

"I know, but you have to. You have school. I'll be fine. I promise. Just go with Ash and get on that plane," I whisper in her ear.

"He was all we had left," she whispers between the sobs.

"I know, but we still have each other," I remind her. This is killing me. My pain is more for her than me.

Our uncle took care of us when no one else was there. When my dad was killed, he took us in. He raised us as his own. Angel doesn't know any different; she was too young to even remember our dad.

"I'll call you when I land," she says pulling away slowly. I let her go with a nod and watch as Ashley pulls her away. My heart sinks in my chest.

"I'm sorry, butterfly." His voice is as soft as silk. I turn to look at him. He opens his arms, a somber invitation that I accept. I step into them and fall apart as he holds me tightly.

"I'm so sorry," he repeats as he runs his hand down my back. Soothing me.

"He was it. Aside from Angel, I have no one left." I cry harder at that thought.

"No," he snaps harshly. He pulls back, gripping my face in his hands.

"You have me, Brooke." His eyes hold so many secrets. Secrets I want, but I know I can't have.

"What are you doing here anyway?" I swallow hard and try to reign in the tears, but it hurts.

"I was ridin' when I saw you standin' there," he admits with a half-smile on his face.

"How did you know it was me?" I ask a little confused.

"I know that ass of yours – I would know it anywhere. I wanted to ask you somethin'," he says, swallowing hard. His jaw tics as he looks at me. He looks so unsure of himself. This is not the Declan I know, but I like seeing this vulnerable side of him.

"What is it?" I ask when he doesn't say anything.

"We have a thing up north. We have to ride out to our sister chapter for a member drive. It'll take a few days. I want you to go with me."

My heart hammers in my chest. I can't go. I have the club. My uncle just died.

"I can't. I'm sorry. The club. My uncle." The words tumble from my mouth before I can think or stop them.

"The club's taken care of and your uncle didn't want a funeral," Declan says softly. My eyes jerk to his. How the fuck did he know that? How is the club taken care of?

"What?" I ask not believing him.

"Tic and Rico are gonna handle the club while we're gone. Your uncle didn't want a funeral. It was in his will," he says as if that makes anything better. I'm so confused.

"How the hell do you know that?" I ask. How the hell does he know what's in my uncle's will?

"I have my ways. Will you go with me?" he asks again.

"I can't...I just...I don't know."

His hands pull me into him. Everything that's happening is all too much, too consuming. I'm overwhelmed. I surrender to the enormity of my new reality and sob into his chest, inhaling the smell of leather and man that I've come to know with Declan.

"Just say yes. It'll all be ok, butterfly, I promise."

I pull back and wipe my eyes. Maybe he's right. Maybe I need this break.

"Ok. Yeah. I'll go." The smile that crosses his face is priceless. I've never seen it before, and I think I might just like it.

"Yeah?" he asks as though he didn't hear me the first time.

"Yeah. I think I need this."

He nods, pulling me back into him. "I need this, too."

Chapter 23
Declan

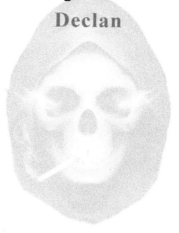

I came back to the clubhouse to get a few things packed up. Brooke sits in the corner in her own little world, completely lost in thought. My heart breaks for her. Her world is slowly coming down around her, and she has nowhere left to turn. Except for me. And that thought scares the hell out of me. I made sure to call the guys after she said her uncle was killed. It took Mystic all of thirty seconds to pull his information and find out he didn't want a funeral. I don't know if I should have let that fact slip in front of her because it is her family but it was the truth. As far as the club goes, the guys wouldn't hesitate to step in and help out while we're gone.

"Let's go get your stuff," I say softly. Her eyes come to meet mine, and it's only then do I realize just how lost she truly is. Her eyes are vacant, nothing more than a shell of the girl I first met.

"I don't know how to do this alone, Dec." Her words come out so softly they are almost a whisper.

"You don't have to, Brooke."

She shakes her head before looking away from me. I walk toward her, determined to make her understand me. Dropping to my knees in front of her, I take her face in my hands.

"I may not be a good man, but I care. I can see the world in those eyes of yours when you aren't sad. You shine brighter than any fuckin' star at night, Brooke. Your attitude, the way you carry yourself - you are stronger than you give yourself credit for, darlin'."

She studies me with an intent gleam in her beautiful dark eyes. Each second of silence is like a stolen breath. It's suffocating.

"I don't know that I am anymore. I used to be strong. I used to want to take on the world just because I could," she says with the hint of a smile.

"You still can, sweetheart. You know deep down that this world is still yours to take. You just have to reach out and grab it."

Her eyes water with unshed tears. "Are you sure you want me to go with you?" she asks as though that is even a possibility.

"Damn right I do. You think I would have asked if I didn't?"

She smiles and pulls her bottom lip between her teeth before looking back at me. "Thank you, Declan."

"For what?"

"For being who you are." The air is knocked from my lungs. No one has ever said that to me. No one aside from this club has respected me for who I am, and now she's thanking me for it? I don't know how to respond. So I don't.

I grab her hand and pull her to her feet.

"Let's go pick up your stuff now," I tell her as I lead her out of my room.

"Brooke! Are you going?" Cherry yells as soon as we step into the main room. Her eyes light up when she sees Brooke. Brooke gives her a small nod.

"She's off limits to you." I point at Cherry, making my warning clear.

"She isn't into me anyway." Cherry smirks and makes Brooke giggle. It's the best sound in the world right now.

"Wait. What?" I look down at a now laughing Brooke. "You ain't into girls?" I ask her.

Brooke looks up at me and shakes her head. "No. We were just fucking with you." She laughs again.

"Way to ruin my fuckin' wet dreams," I say.

Brooke punches me in the arm before laughing harder. "I needed that laugh. Thank you." She smiles up at me again.

"You have got to stop thankin' me for things I want to give you."

Her smile slowly fades. I drop my bag to the floor. I can see the wheels spinning in her mind.

"You don't even know me," she whispers.

"I don't care, I know enough. I know that I love your heart. I know that you can fight like a goddamn man. I know that you will fight like hell to get what you want. You take care of those that you love. You have a light that can brighten even the dark days. There's so much more to you that I want. I've never wanted to know a woman, not unless she was in my bed, and that's as far as it went. You…fuck, butterfly. You make me see things in a different light, and I'm not sure how to handle th-"

Before I can even finish the sentence, she pushes up, pressing her lips to mine. The taste of her salty tears still lingers. I take them all. One by one, I kiss them away until there's just her.

"Fuck me! I'd like to get behind that." Mayhem's voice comes out of nowhere.

"Let me touch it." He steps up behind Brooke, his hands roaming closely to her ass. I cut my eyes at him, but I don't need to do anything. Brooke spins around, slamming her fist into his stomach. I watch him gasp and cough.

"Now that's my girl!" I roar with pride. She can handle herself pretty well. This week is going to be all about us, getting to know each other. I want to know her. I want to know why fighting is her thing. Hell, I want to know where she learned it.

"If that wasn't so fuckin' sexy, I'd be pissed." Mayhem stands up and grins like a fool at her.

"I didn't mean to hurt you," Brooke says with a smirk.

"Oh, baby. You can hit me, kick me, beat me - I don't give a shit. That was sexy as fuck."

I roll my eyes at Mayhem. He's such a loose cannon you never know how he's going to react to something like that.

"Let's get the fuck outta here. I'm ready for this member drive," I say, grabbing Brooke's hand. I lead her outside when Tic looks over.

"She goin'?" he asks, and I nod in response.

"What the fuck? I gotta get left back, and she gets to go?"

I almost laugh at the motherfucker.

"You the VP?" I ask him. He shakes his head.

"Then you follow orders, princess. You don't like it, step the fuck down," I growl. Tic may be Blu's son, but he doesn't get treated any differently. He knows his role here just like any of the others do.

"Have a good one," he says over his shoulder.

"He's friendly," Brooke mocks.

"He's a good guy. He just gets tired of his daddy tellin' him what to do." She looks up at me when I say that.

"Blu's his dad. He and Mayhem are brothers. Different moms." Her mouth drops open much like everyone's does when they find that out.

"They are so different," she says in astonishment.

"Oh, yeah. A hell of a lot different. Mayhem is out there. Well, you see that shit. Tic, he's a little more reserved than his brother."

"That's by a long shot."

Chapter 24

Brooke

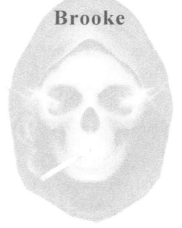

The ride to Norther California was nice. We stopped a few times to take a break, but I've loved being on the back of Dec's bike. It gives me a sense of freedom I've never felt before. It makes me feel alive when everything inside of me wants to shut down and give up.

Declan went to check us into the hotel where we will be staying. He said the clubhouse the guys have up here is smaller than theirs and wouldn't accommodate everyone. I stand here on the beach looking out at the crashing waves. The colors are bouncing off the water. A peaceful feeling surrounds me.

"I know you're always with me," I say mostly to myself, hoping my uncle is somewhere out there in the clouds. My chest aches from the loss of someone as special as he was. He was everything that we needed for so long, and now it's just me.

"Your uncle would want you to be at peace, not crumblin' into pieces." His voice is warm and soothing. I was so lost in my own thougts I hadn't heard him come out here.

"I know. I'm trying Declan. I never had to do anything alone before. If I didn't have my uncle, I had Angel."

I glance over my shoulder, watching as his eyes glistening in the sunlight. He knows about me, but I still don't know much about him. I want to know what makes him tick, about his past, about his life, about his mom.

"Tell me about her."

I take him in. He's beautiful. He's perfect, a big heart hidden from the rest of the world. So why would he even care about someone like me?

"Why me, Declan?" I ask because I need to know. I don't see it. I can't. Declan licks his lips before moving to stand in front of me.

"My mom was a good woman. Loyal to the club and my dad. She was like you. She was a light. She was a leader. She didn't take anyone's shit." He looks off to the side for a second like he's remembering her. "She made her own path no matter what people said. People would tell her she wasn't worth shit bein' a biker's wife. She proved them all wrong. I see that in you. No matter what people tell you, there's more in there. Not everyone will get to see it. Not everyone will care that it's in there."

Declan looks back over at me, and I raise my hand to stop him. Because I know what he sees. And I can feel it.

"You see it." It isn't a question. I know he can. Whether I like it or not, Dec pushes me. He pushes my limits, my boundaries to see how far I can go.

"Yeah. I see a lot in you, butterfly." His eyes move between mine before he leans down, capturing my lips with his. It's the softest of kisses that makes my knees weak. Declan's hand wraps around my waist, pulling me closer. His kiss intensifies. I'm a panting mess when he pulls away from me.

"There's a lot of things that happen in my world that I don't want you to be a part of..." he starts but doesn't finish.

"Your world isn't mine, Dec. You are though. You are a part of my world." My words must surprise him. He stands there staring at me like he has more to say, but no words form.

"You can't have me without the club. The club is who I am. I'm afraid that what you might see and learn about me will scare you off. That's the last thing I want to happen," he admits, causing my heart to swell.

"I don't think you can scare me that easily." I wrap my arms around his waist and hold on tightly. Declan sighs before pressing his lips into the top of my head.

"I'm gonna hold you to that, darlin'," he whispers into my hair.

We stand there holding each other for a long time. Neither of us speak, but I don't think that words are needed. We have an undeniable connection. One I want to explore, but the fear of losing anyone else holds me back. Fear that I may screw up something so good. I've become so focused on taking care of the club and Angel that I don't know how to deal with a relationship.

"Let's go get some dinner. I wanna feed you, and then I wanna fuck you," Dec says with lust in his voice. I pull away and look up at him.

"You're amazing, you know that?"

My words elicit a good laugh from him before he kisses me again. He grabs my hand and pulls me toward the hotel.

"I don't think I'm that amazin'. I'm just me. I am what this world made me, and if you can accept that, then I'm happy," he admits but won't look at me. I know that had to be hard for him to share. He keeps his emotions under tight control, never showing anyone too much.

"I think I can handle you. I mean, I did kick you that once," I say with a coy smile on my face.

"Yeah, about that. Payback is a motherfucker. And you haven't been on the recievin' end of that yet." He chuckles.

"Oh, I don't think you have the skills to take me, my VP." His eyes find mine, and that's where they stay.

"Say it again," he says softly.

I furrow my brows and repeat it. "My VP." His eyes glisten as he stares down at me.

"Can we go swimming?" I ask when his stare becomes too much to handle. The intensity makes me too uncomfortable. I want to throw myself into his arms. Hold him tighter than I should. Declan blinks rapidly before shaking his head with a smile.

"Of course. We can do whatever you want."

Chapter 25

Declan

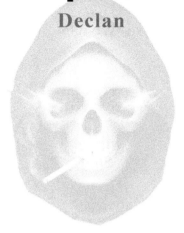

When we walked into the in-house restaurant I noticed it was nice as hell. We are in a fucking five-star hotel so I expect as much. We don't fit in here, which is why most of the guys went out to eat. It makes me feel a little on edge. My body is a little tenser than usual, but I wanted Brooke to have a good time, and I knew they were having live music here tonight.

"You look so different," she says as she keeps smiling at me. I love the way her eyes light up, the way her smile has brightened.

"Was I so bad before?" I asked giving her a smirk.

"No. You know you're hot. I've just never seen you without the cut and all that." Her eyes travel over my plain black button-down shirt. What? I can't go all preppy on her! This right here is something I reserve for funerals.

"You look good too," I tell her. Her cheeks flush at my compliment. She's not usually like this. She doesn't always let her emotions show on her face so I blame it on the amount of wine that she's already consumed.

"Thank you. For all of this."

"I said no more thank yous. I'm glad you're here," I tell her honestly. I was hoping she'd come. In fact, when I went to ride around town I was thinking of how to ask her. Saying the words out loud was harder than I thought it would be but I knew I wanted her to come along. I'd never had a real relationship before Brooke. This is all new to me.

"What was your mom like?" she asks me. My heart leaps a little. It's a strange concept for me to talk to someone else about her. She knows some minimal details about my mom, but I want to share more with her. That's the kind of person Brooke is; she makes you feel safe. You want to tell her things because you know you can trust her with it.

"She was a great mom. She did everything she could for me. She tried to raise me to be a better man than my dad wanted to." Brooke watches me, her glass of wine in her hand. For some reason, looking at Brooke makes it easier for me to talk about my mom. The pain and loss seems much less when she's close.

Her beauty, this setting – it's like something out of a movie. This isn't what I'd expected when I asked her to come with me.

"What happened to her?"

"She was shot and killed." I take a deep breath before I can continue. The images of my mother are too fresh in my mind. " I was with her when it happened. I was twelve at the time. Watchin' her lie there and bleed to death, it killed me. My dad went crazy. He became distant and even more violent. He ended up making bad moves for the club. Understandable since she was the love of his life. After that, he raised me to be what I am today - he made me into the man I am."

She takes a sip of her wine before setting the glass on the table. Her eyes are glossy like she wants to cry for me, for my situation but she doesn't. She holds it back.

"What about your parents?" I ask. I see the look. She's closing me out. She doesn't trust me enough to give me that information, even if I did just give mine to her.

"Dance with me," she says, her eyes looking haunted. I let her avoid the subject for now. I nod once and stand before taking her hand in mine, pulling her from the chair. I walk us to the dance floor, not really giving a shit that everyone is staring at us. With all my tattoos and shit, I can't say that I blame them. But this isn't about them; this is Brooke and me. I wrap my arm around her waist and pull her closer to my body. She throws her arms around my neck, holding on tightly.

"You know everyone is staring at us," she whispers.

I chuckle before I say, "Let them stare. We're makin' magic right now."

Brooke pulls back, staring up at me with wide eyes. "Are we?" she says softly, the hint of a smile tugging at the corner of her lips.

"Yeah, we are, baby." I lean down and press my lips to hers. You can feel it. The magic of this moment. It surrounds us.

Our lips dance to their own song as our bodies do the same. Everything about her feels right, but there's something off since our conversation and it's nagging at the back of my mind. I feel like she's trying to avoid something from her past. Her focus has drifted. I break our kiss and pull her into my chest. I need to get her back in a good place. This night is going too perfectly for it to end with her regretting coming with me. I want that connection that we've had to linger with us the rest of the night so I change the subject.

"What did you want to be when you were younger?" I ask.

"I wanted to be a princess, like any other girl my age." She giggles softly.

"You are a princess. My princess."

"So, you're my prince?" She pulls back enough to look up at me.

"I can be anything you want me to be," I tell her. It's true, and I mean it. She makes me feel that way, like I can do or be anything in the fucking world. It's an amazing feeling to have, too.

"I just want you to be you, Dec."

I swallow hard. How she has this effect on me, I will never understand, but I like it. It's some more of that magic that makes us, us.

I lean in and tell her, "I wanna take you to our room."

"And do what exactly?" She's playing with me, and my dick is loving it. When the words leave her mouth, I'm instantly relaxed that my playful Brooke has come back.

"First, I wanna take all your clothes off. Then I want to kiss every inch of your skin." Her breathing picks up. Fuck, I love that I am the one who can make her react like that, make her feel these things.

"Then what?" she asks, her breathing coming heavier.

"Then I want to lick you until you call out my name."

"Then?" God, look at her. So, fucking turned on by my words.

"Then I wanna pull your fuckin' hair so hard that it hurts and plunge into you so goddamn deep that I will mark you for days." I can see the red cross her cheeks. The way her body shudders slightly. She's horny.

"So, why don't you do it?" she asks breathlessly with a quirk of her brow.

I grin devilishly at her before I say, "Nope. I want dessert first."

Brooke's mouth hangs open before she punches me in the chest.

Chapter 26

Brooke

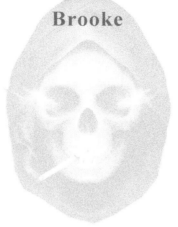

Declan has teased me to no end. I sit here watching him shovel cake into his mouth like he's a kid. I don't know how the hell he does it, but he makes even that look sexy. He grins at me, but I swear to God I'm about to kick his ass if he doesn't hurry up. I can't control the way my body heats from the inside out. I'm squirming in my chair like a kid waiting for recess.

"I have to go to the bathroom," I finally say. He sets his fork down and looks at me.

"Liar."

"I'm not!"

"Yeah, you are. I bet you're tryin' to get yourself off. Touchin' that clit which belongs to me." The gruff way he says it sends heat spiraling through my body.

"Declan," I start to whine. He just smiles and chuckles. I start to shove myself up, but his large hand clamps down on my knee.

"Don't you dare fuckin' touch your pussy. That belongs to me now," he says through gritted teeth.

"You are driving me crazy, Declan," I say my mood getting pissier by the second.

"Good, that's what I wanted to do. Your orgasms come from me." His fingers stay clamped around my knee as he takes another drink of his beer.

"This is stupid. Let go of me." My frustration is reaching new heights. I try to move his hand when he inches it higher, closer to where I want him to touch me. The shudders that rack my body are going to be noticed by others if he doesn't stop.

"Declan," I warn him. He just gives me that sexy grin.

"What, baby?" Look at him saying baby to me right now.

"Don't you dare 'baby' me. If you don't get up and take me upstairs to our room and fuck me, I will find someone else to do it." His eyes blaze with hunger, but I can see the hint of rage in them.

"You ever let anyone touch what belongs to me, and I will fuckin' kill them," he growls. He stands quickly, throwing some cash onto the table, and grabs my hand. He practically yanks me out of my chair and drags me through the restaurant toward the elevator.

"What's wrong? Can't handle me?" I ask. I know I'm pushing him. I know I'm getting a rise out of him, and I love it. I can feel the way his hand clenches and unclenches around mine.

"You askin' for me to spank your ass, butterfly?" He looks down at me as my heart picks up a beat.

"I don't ask for anything," I tell him. The desire dances off him. All I want is to wrap my legs around his waist and fuck him right here in the lobby.

"I know that look," he says playfully.

"What look is that?" I ask like nothing happened.

"You want me right here and now, don't you?"

"You think too highly of yourself, Dec."

As soon as the elevator doors open, he lifts me in his arms. He steps in, pinning my body to the wall.

"I think highly of myself?" he asks, his lips hovering so close to mine. I'd give anything for him just to kiss me but I know he won't.

"Yeah. You do," I tease him. In response, his hips move, grinding against me. My body responds, ready to take everything he's about to give me.

"You don't know shit, butterfly," he mumbles before kissing me roughly. His tongue dives into my mouth, taking what he wants from me. I can feel just how hard he is right now. As fast as our kiss started, he stops it. He sets me on my feet and backs away slowly.

"What are you doing?" I ask him as I pant.

He doesn't speak; he just gives me an evil grin.

"You wanna play, butterfly? Let's play." The way he looks at me is about to be my undoing. I want this man more than I should.

I take a step toward him when the doors open, making room for another couple to climb in. I retreat to my side, his eyes burning into me the whole time. Unable to read anything in his heated gaze, I quietly endure the rest of the ride. When the elevator stops on our floor, Declan tilts his head so I know to get off. He follows behind me, staying at least three feet away, but never once does he touch me. His presence can be felt, but I want the warmth of him to envelope me like it always does when he's close.

"Five Sixteen," he grumbles. I look up and check the room numbers as I go. Almost there and I plan on jumping his ass when I get to it. Fuck this game he wants to play.

I stand off to the side when I reach our room, allowing him to unlock and open the door. As soon as he does, I jump. Slamming into him, I damn near climb his body. His hands wrap around my ass, digging in painfully. I love feeling him against me. Touching me.

"This what you been waitin' for?" he asks, walking us toward the bed. I nod once before my mouth is back on his. He doesn't stop either as he lowers us onto the bed.

"This shirt," I whine as I try to pull it off him.

Chapter 27

Declan

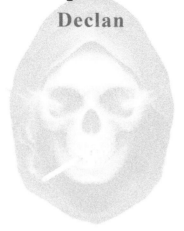

I love the fact that she can't get me undressed fast enough, but I don't plan on letting her have her own way. She needs to learn who is in charge here, and regardless of what she might think, it isn't her. She throws my shirt to the floor, but that's all I'm giving her. I pull back and stare down at her flushed cheeks, her body writhing and wanting more.

"What are you doing?" she demands, her eyes burning with need.

"You think you control everything. I'm gonna teach you a little lesson."

Her eyes flicker with rage and anger. She can pout and fuss all she wants, but she isn't getting it. She may want control, but it's mine.

"Don't you dare play games with me right now," she says in that little pissed off tone of hers. I watch her hand slowly slide into the front of her pants.

"I'll walk away if you keep that up," I say with a nod toward her hand. She watches me, trying to decide if I'll really do it.

"You wouldn't," she says in a strong voice, shoulders thrown back.

"Keep touchin' yourself and watch me leave."

She seems to be warring with herself. Deep down she has to know I'll do it. I don't fuck around, and she knows this. I watch as Brooke slowly pulls her hand free of her jeans, but that's only so she can slide the jeans down her legs and off her body. She lies there in nothing at all. Her pussy is on display, and my dick is screaming for a piece of her.

"You think that changes things?" I ask casually, trying to sound unaffected. She locks eyes with me, and I can see that she's trying to reign in her anger. She wants the control that I'm not willing to give her.

"Why are you doing this to me?" she questions in an almost whiny tone.

"'Cause you want everything your way. I told you, that's not how this works." I give her a cocky grin before I climb on the end of the bed. I slowly part her legs, leaning down to run my tongue up her thigh. Brooke gasps but I know what she really wants. I move up her body until she's writhing on the bed beneath me. Her back arches, her eyes close.

"Is this so bad?" I ask her before licking a long stroke over her wetness. Brooke moans in response. I chuckle against her before I spread those pink lips and get to work on her pussy. I've never tasted her like this before. We've always had quick, hard fucks here and there, but this is what I want. I want to take my time and drive her insane. I want her body to react to my every touch. I want her screaming my name. My tongue tortures her pussy. She is every man's wet dream. She's perfect. Her hands slide into my hair, tugging and yanking, trying to get me closer.

"Please, Dec," she pleads as her body tenses up.

I love it. Her begging me to let her come. That's how it should be. I stick my tongue inside her, and God fucking help me, I almost cum in my jeans. The taste of her has me on edge. I work her clit in hard, rough circles with my fingers while my tongue strokes the softness inside of her.

Brooke screams and pulls my hair as she releases all that pent-up energy. I lick and suck at everything that comes out of her. I fucking love this. I slow my licks down as I hold her hips in my hands to steady her while her orgasm slowly begins to fade. When she's panting and relaxed, I sit up and pull my jeans off.

"Now you can have what you want," I say as I yank them down my legs with my boxers.I grab a condom and put it on quickly before kicking my jeans to the floor. Her eyes travel my body and the hunger in this is almost overwhelming.

"You like what you see?" I ask. Her eyes come to meet mine, and a slow smile crosses her face.

"I've never seen anything as perfect as you." The words come out softly, but I hear them.

The dynamics of this little fuck fest we're having are beginning to change. I can feel it deep inside of me. Brooke's becoming more than just a hot piece of ass that I want to fuck senseless. She's becoming way more, and it scares the shit out of me.

I position myself between her legs before shoving into her slowly. Her legs lock around my waist, holding me in place. I look down into her eyes and see my feelings reflected back at me. It's the strangest feeling to experience, but I know she's going to end up meaning more to me than I originally thought she would.

"What are you thinkin'?" I ask her as I slowly roll my hips. I reach up with one hand and gently brush a strand of hair away from her face. Now that all of the urgent tension has been expelled, things have taken a slower, softer tone between us.

"I don't know what I feel anymore." She doesn't need to say the words. I know she's talking about us. I know because I have that exact same problem.

My hips roll, causing her eyes flutter, but I never thrust too hard. I want to take my time and watch her come undone for me. I want to see the way I affect her.

"I know what you mean."

Her eyes come back to mine, the look of shock shining brightly in them. "So, now what?" she says with a gasp when I hit that spot she loves.

"Now, I make you cum all over me. Now we see where this thing between us is goin'."

A smile crosses her beautiful face and I lose myself in her.

Chapter 28

Brooke

"What is all this?" I ask looking at all the people milling around this clubhouse. It's nicer than the one where Declan lives.

"We're gettin' new recruits in. A few guys from another chapter and some are Nomads. Probably pick up a few new prospects, too," Declan says as I look around. There are so many people that it's hard to keep straight who is who.

"Yo, Declan!" I hear a man roar behind us. Dec turns to face him, never letting go of me.

"Goddamn, Brick! It's been a long time, brother," Dec says before releasing his grip on me to hug his friend. Watching him is amazing. The way his eyes light up when he sees his family. That's what they are. Just like he said, they are family. You can see it in their eyes.

"Fuck, been what? Like three years?" Brick, says pulling back.

"Somethin' like that. How you been? How're the girls?" Declan asks as he throws his arm around my shoulder. My chest swells with pride. It makes me feel safe and cared for. It's strange that I'd even want that, but with Declan, it feels right.

"Gettin' big, brother. Karrie's goin' to high school this year. I don't know where the time goes," Brick says.

"Goddamn! Can't believe that shit." Declan smiles and pulls me in closer.

"So, who's this?" Brick nods toward me.

"This is my girl, Brooke." He thrusts me toward his friend unexpectedly. Brick grabs my hand and smiles.

"How'd you do it?" he asks me with a twinkle in his eye.

"I don't know what you mean," I say, unsure how I'm supposed to respond to him.

"How'd you get ol' Dec there to settle down? Last I knew him, he was all over everything with legs."

A blush creeps up my cheeks. I can feel it. Declan grabs me and yanks me back against him with a growl.

"She's good to me. Don't need to look anywhere else," Dec says.

I glance up at him, and I see what looks like pride in his eyes. Does he really think that much of me? We haven't known each other long, but I suppose I feel the same about him.

"Heard that! Let's get some food. I heard the boys were settin' up a ring out back. You gettin' in on those fights?" Brick asks Declan.

My eyes shoot to his. Does he fight too? He's never told me that.

"Maybe. I haven't decided yet." Declan winks at me before pulling me with him in the opposite direction of Brick.

"There's a lot of people here," I say.

"Nervous?" Dec looks down and asks me. I shake my head. Nothing bothers me. Not in a long time. The only thing that seems to affect me anymore is Declan himself.

"You hungry? You want a beer?" he asks.

I love the way he looks at me. I nod once, and he leans down to kiss my cheek. "Stay right here." The little growl didn't go unnoticed.

I grin as I watch him make his way around everyone. The way they stop him to talk. The way his whole presence just demands attention. He carries a huge amount of authority around with him, and it's amazing to see the respect that he's given.

"Who are you here with?"

I turn my head when I see a little blonde wearing barely anything. I look her up and down before I answer her. "Declan."

"Seriously?" she asks, seeming to be interested. I don't know much about these club girls, but I have a feeling I'm about to find out real quick.

"Yeah, seriously. Why is that so hard to believe?" I snap. She smiles, and I swear I want to shove my fist down her throat.

"Declan doesn't bring anyone to these things." She flips her hair over her shoulder but doesn't stop smiling.

"Well, he did this time."

Her eyes come to meet mine and a hint of anger filters into view. I love it. That's my kind of thing.

"You don't know who you're talking to right now." Her smile fades, her hands clenching at her sides.

"I'd say the same to you." I turn toward her and square off my shoulders.

"We can handle this outside," she snaps.

"Gladly." Oh shit. I'm going to have to beat this bitch's ass right here in front of everyone.

Chapter 29

Declan

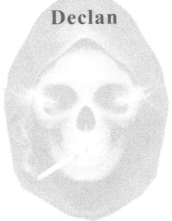

I found us some food and drinks, but when I went back to the spot I left Brooke, she wasn't there.

"Hey, Mayhem. You seen, Brooke?" I call out to him. He shakes his head when I spot Cherry.

"Cherry Bear!" I call out to her. She turns on her heel and comes straight toward me.

"What's up, Declan?" she asks with a smile.

"Have you seen Brooke? I went to get food, and she was gone when I came back," I tell her. My nerves are firing off. She isn't claimed, which means she fair game to anyone here. The thought of someone coming near her pisses me off royally.

I don't want to fight a brother, but for her, I will. The thought alone shakes me up.

"No. I'll go look though." Cherry sees the concern in my eyes. Or the rage. Either way, she hurries the hell off to look for her.

I can hear the guys cheering and shit. They must have already started the fights out back. Maybe she went to watch. I head toward the door when Cherry comes rushing back in it.

"Found her!" she says with a giant ass grin on her face.

"Where?" I set the food down but keep my beer in hand. Cherry nods toward the ring, and that's when I see her. My butterfly is standing there in a tank top and her short jean shorts. Her hands are clenched, her focus is on point. I've never seen her like this before - so poised and ready. I shove my way to the front of the crowd and take her in.

"You know the new girl?" Dusty, one of the local brothers, ask. I look over at him and nod.

"Yeah, that's my girl," I say with pride. I turn back to the ring and watch as she throws jab after jab.

"Who is that?" I ask Dusty, nodding toward the other girl.

"Kelp's old lady. He's a local brother. Not sure you've met him yet. She's a scrapper."

I chuckle under my breath because I know Brooke can handle herself. The fists fly, and I stand here in awe of her. She looks like she's in her element. The way she moves with such precision and skill, I fucking love it.

The guys are going insane over the fight. I can't say that I blame them either. Two hot bitches in the ring is a sight to behold.

"Fuck yeah, baby!" I scream when the other chick hits the mat. A few of the guys move in and check her, but it's Brooke who surprises me. She's at the girl's side on the mat next to her, whispering in her ear. The girl nods and gives her a thumbs up and a smile. They pick Kelp's old lady up and stand her on her feet as the crowd surrounding the ring goes insane.

Brooke glances around anxiously until her eyes lock with mine. She looks nervous and unsure of herself. I smile and give her a little nod, and I can see her visibly relax. Pride surges through me as I hold out my arms to her. Brooke wastes no time climbing out of the ring and leaping her sweaty body into them. I spin her around as I hold her tightly.

"That was fuckin' amazin', darlin'. I've never seen you like that," I tell her, pride evident in my voice. She pulls her head from my shoulder and gazes up at me. In this fucking second, I know everything is changing. I knew it was but this - this is different.

"You mean a lot to me, Declan," she says softly. Her truth shines brightly from her eyes. Her words and her eyes create a world where there's no one else but us; it's like the rest of the crowd just disappears. She holds me captive. She sucks the air from my lungs. She makes me feel whole. I lean my head down and kiss her roughly, letting her know what she means to me, too.

Our moment is broken when I hear who I assume to be Kelp bitching behind us. I set Brooke on her feet before I spin around to face him. I push Brooke instinctively behind me.

"What's the problem?" I ask. Kelp is looking mighty pissed off at the moment. It's almost laughable that he'd be pissed about his woman getting her ass handed to her by mine.

"She ain't an old lady! That shit was uncalled for and needs to be handled!" he roars as he points at Brooke. I cross my arms over my chest and glare at him.

"You mad your girl got her ass handed to her? Don't take that shit out on her." I nod over my shoulder at Brooke.

"You know the rules, Declan!" he snaps. I do know the rules, but that means shit to me at the moment.

"So, what the fuck you wanna do here, Kelp?" I asked, straightening my back. He knows I'll take his ass on. They all know it.

"She ain't a old lady, and she put her hands on somethin' that belongs to the club!" he roars louder. Kelp is such a goddamn prick. He couldn't just take that shit and walk.

"What's your plan on this, Declan?" I glance over at Blu wondering where the hell he came from.

"She's mine," I snap.

His eyes find mine before he says, "You claimin' her?"

I look over my shoulder at the wide eyes of Brooke. I bring my gaze back to Blu's and say, "You're goddamn right I am."

Chapter 30

Brooke

Declan drug my ass out of that party as soon as he finished talking to Blu. I was shocked, too. I was actually having a good time with the fight and all. He hasn't said a word since we got back to the hotel. It makes me uneasy, nervous.

I sent a quick text to Ash and Angel to make sure they were doing ok. Losing my uncle has brought into perspective the importance of family. I never thought about it the way I am right now. Ash and Angel are all I have left, and I find that I am holding them closer than ever before.

Watching Dec sit out on the patio with his head in his hands is bothering me more than I thought it would. He looks so lost, like he doesn't know what to do with himself. It's not a look I'm used to seeing on him. My heart roars in my ears as I walk out the door behind him. He doesn't look up. He doesn't move. I rest my hands on his shoulders, and I can feel him relax into my touch.

"Are you ok? I didn't mean to start any trouble," I say softly. I truly didn't. She mentioned fighting, and I went with it. I had no idea it was against some kind of rules they had.

"Wasn't your fault. She knew the rules," he says, but he still won't look up at me.

"If I messed up, Declan, I'm sorry." I start to pull my hands away from him when his reaches up and covers mine. His warmth is soothing in ways I never knew I wanted or needed to be soothed.

"You didn't; I did. I shouldn't have walked away from you." He pulls my hands, so I move to stand in front of him.

"Then what's wrong?" I ask, seeing the torn look in his eyes.

"I made things more complicated, Brooke. If I didn't, hell would have been rained down on you."

He shakes his head at his words, maybe his thoughts, but I'm still confused. I don't understand what has caused him to be like this. Pulling my hands from his, I grip his face and lift his face up to me. He finally looks up at me, and I hate the look I see.

"What do you mean? This is all new to me, Dec. Tell me."

Declan sighs before pulling me into his lap. I snuggle in close as he starts to talk.

"You know when Blu asked me if I was claimin' you?" he asks, his voice stuttering a little.

"Yeah."

"Do you know what that means?"

"No. I don't know what any of that means, Dec." I try to move, but he doesn't let me. He holds me tighter.

"It means you're mine now. You're club property. You're my property." The way he says it sends a chill up my spine. His property? What the hell does that even mean?

"What does that mean?" I ask mostly to myself.

Declan pushes me gently off his lap before he stands, running his hand through his hair. He's frustrated. I can see it in his face, his body – hell, I can feel it.

"Declan?" I say before he looks over at me, a new heat building in his eyes.

"It means that you're mine! Mine to take care of. Mine to protect. Mine to have. Mine to love!" He roars with each word that comes out of his mouth. My heart thunders in my chest as I let that sink in.

"You do that anyway," I say softly, my eyes never leaving his. His reality isn't that bad. It's what he does now. He takes care of me. He protects me.

"You don't get it. It also makes you a goddamn target for any other club that wants a war! You are a goddamn walkin' target now because of me!" He slams his fist into the brick wall, tearing apart his skin. I watch as the blood flows down his hand. Declan doesn't seem to notice it, though. He's lost in a world that he didn't want me to be a part of.

"So, tell them to forget it! You don't want me, that's fine! Tell them I'm nothing to you!" I yell.

He doesn't look up at me. He stands there, his breathing coming rapidly. His anger rolls off him in waves.

"Go tell them you don't want me!" I scream once more. I turn to head back inside with tears prickling my eyes. I don't cry. I won't, and I sure as fuck won't let him see how he is affecting me.

"I can't fuckin' do that!" he roars.

Getting a grip on my emotions, I turn back to see him watching me.

"Why not? It's just a few words. Tell them you weren't thinking when you said it." I reason it out with him. He's having an internal war, and I hate to see him like this. It kills a piece of me inside to watch that look om his face.

"I can't do that," he growls.

"Why not!"

"Because I want you, Brooke! Goddamn it! I want you! I want you to be my old lady! I want to protect you and take care of you! I. Want. You." he says pronouncing each word slowly but firmly.

His eyes dance with danger. He's dangerous. I know that much, but the thought of being his? That settles something deep inside of me. A craving, a need. A need to feel that I belong to someone. To something. Declan has always made me feel special. This is no different. The time that we've spent together have been the most amazing times of my life.

"You said I was a walking target now. What's that mean?" I ask, needing some kind of answers.

Declan runs his hand through his hair before he sighs. "Rival clubs. Anyone who wants to come after us, after me. They will use you to get to me. I never wanted that for you. You deserve better than that!" he thunders.

"I can handle myself, I've been taking care of myself for a long before you showed up, Declan. This isn't any different." I snap. I walk back inside, and I'm surprised when Declan didn't follow me. God, how I wanted him to follow me.

When I realize he doesn't, I change into my bikini and text Cherry. I storm from the room and head outside. I want some time to just enjoy being here. I need a break, some time to not worry about the club, the past - nothing.

"You ok?" Cherry asks when she walks up next to me. Jesus, that girl is hot as fuck in a bikini. Plus, she's sweet as pie, too. Cherry pie. I'm too funny. My inner dialogue brings a smile to my face.

"Just life. Come on. Play in the water with me." I nudge her shoulder. Cherry smiles before running toward the shore. She leaps into the water, screaming and laughing. It pulls at everything inside of me. I want to be that carefree. I want to be that open and happy. Doing as best as I can in the moment, I wade out into the water and sidle up next to her.

"You got a peeper." She pulls me into her arms, hugging me while she whispers in my ear.

I turn my head slightly and look up to see the shadow of Declan on the patio with a cigarette hanging from his lips. I'd love to get inside his head. I'd love to know why he thinks the way he does.

"Are we supposed to be swimming at night?" I wonder out loud. Cherry's laughter pulls my attention back to her.

"Who gives a shit!"

Chapter 31

Declan

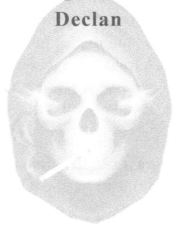

"How'd the drive go?" Tic asks as I take down another shot of vodka.

"Good. Guys will be down in a few days." I'm being short with him, but I don't care. I don't want to talk about shit right now. My head's a goddamn mess. I've made a huge fucking mess of this shit with Brooke, and I have no idea how to clear it up.

"Good to hear. Heard about what happened with your girl. Glad to know she can hold her own."

I glance over and the thought of punching him in the face hits me hard. I growl, letting him know that I'm done talking about this shit.

"Dec! Get in here," Blu hollers over the music.

I shove off the stool and head into the office before dropping into the chair across from his desk.

"Do you know why you're my VP?" he asks me.

I look up at him like he's a goddamn puzzle. What the fuck kind of question is that?

"'Cause my dad was the Prez once?" I ask with a sarcastic tone.

"Fuck you, Declan. You're the goddamn VP 'cause we all know you can do it. This ain't got anything to do with your dad, and you know it," he snaps at me.

"What's this about, Blu?" I ask. I'm tired of hearing shit already.

"We have an issue. I just got word that the assholes who roughed Brooke up a little while back at the club were Dragon MC."

My eyes shoot to his and hold there. No fucking way. They don't make any moves this far west.

"They're out of Alabama. What the fuck are they doin' around here?" I ask him, my anger beginning to make my blood boil.

"You ain't gonna like this," he says before blowing out a breath. "Your dad had a run in with them when he was Prez. Things got shitty, but that's not the reason they're around. Seems Brooke's daddy was a dirty cop."

What the fuck?

I shoot out of my chair. My hands land on my hips as I let that sink in. What in the fuck! How didn't I know her dad was a cop?! Of all the fucking girls in the goddamn world, mine would be the daughter of a cop! I can't even wrap my brain around it.

"I know you got questions, but I don't have all the answers just yet. I got Mystic on it now. So far all we can tell is that Devon had some kind of run-in with them. Not sure where that leaves the club."

A fucking *cop*!

Those words are burned into my mind. They are there and will never leave. Her dad was a fucking cop. Why didn't she ever tell me that? Why did she keep that part of her life a secret?

"Calm the fuck down, brother. She had her reasons, I'm sure."

I cut my eyes to Blu's. "A cop, Blu! That means she knows more fuckin' cops!" I roar.

"It doesn't mean shit. Her daddy was killed when she was little. Devon wasn't a part of the force, and he's the one who raised her," he says, trying to be the voice of reason when the fucking situation has none.

I shake my head. That doesn't mean shit. That means nothing at all. Cops are a lot like MCs; they have a brotherhood that they honor and protect. If her dad was really a cop, she knows more of them.

"You know how fucked this whole situation just got?" I ask him, tugging at my hair.

"No. I don't. If it's fucked, you're the one fuckin' it. I don't see an issue with Brooke. She's never brought shit to our doorstep. From what Mystic can dig up, she has nothin' to do with the force either," Blu snaps.

This is bullshit. She should have told me! I'm getting more pissed by the second. I run my hand down my face when Blu interrupts my inner rant.

"Why don't you ask her, Dec. You ain't never backed down before. You care about that girl. Don't let your stubborn ass fuck up somethin' good." He stands up, points at me, and proceeds to stomp past me and out of the office.

My stomach feels like I ate a load of lead. My chest is tight. How didn't I know this? How didn't I know that she was the daughter of a fucking cop? I head out of the office and out the front door. Like Blu said, I need to talk to her about it. I walk down the block completely lost in my own thoughts. I don't know why it should matter to me. She cares about me. I care about her. That's all that should matter, but in my world, that's just not enough. It puts me, the club, and our way of life at risk.

**

I knock on the door and wait. Ashley opens it with a smile.

"Well, well, well. If it isn't the biker who stole my girl's heart." She says. My heart swells hearing those words. I want Brooke's, heart. I want all of her.

"She here?" I ask. Ashley shakes her head.

"She's not at home?" she asks me. Home? What the fuck? I thought this was her home?

"She don't live here?" I ask, getting annoyed. This was where I fucked her with the gun!

"No. I do. She lives across the street, and by the looks of the curtain, she isn't there." Ashley looks around me. I follow her gaze, but I don't get the curtain thing.

"What the fuck does the curtain mean?" I ask. Ashley looks like she doesn't want to tell me at first, but then she softens.

"Ever since she was little, Brooke would leave me a sign. The blue curtain in the living room. When it's open, she isn't home. When it's closed, she is, and if it's half way, there's something wrong," she finally tells me.

I open my mouth, but I don't have anything to say. What the hell do you say to that?

"She was afraid that someone would come after her and her sister after her dad was killed. They never found out who it was, and it bothered her. That house was her dad's. He left it all to her, and once she turned eighteen, she moved back into it. She and Angel lived with Devon when they were younger," she explains.

"And she still does the curtain thing?" I ask.

"Yeah. It's our little way of making sure she's ok. She puts up a good front, but I know things still bother her," Ashley adds.

"Well, fuck. I need to talk to her. You know where she might be?" I ask. Ashley nods.

"You know that gym over on Alpine? She works out there most days. If she isn't there, she's at the club."

"Thanks, Ashley. Not just for the information but for lookin' out for her." It makes me happy to know she has Ashley. She's a good friend.

"You really care about her, don't you?" she asks when I turn to walk away.

I glance back over my shoulder and say, "Yeah. A hell of a lot more than I should."

Chapter 32

Brooke

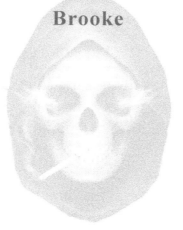

I've pushed myself harder than I have in a long time. The trip with Declan weighs heavily on my mind. It's been a few weeks since we've been back. I haven't seen him or made an attempt to, but neither has he. I know how torn he was about everything that happened while we were up there. It hasn't slipped my mind, though. It's a constant nagging reminder. I care about Declan, but I'm not sure if being mixed up in his club life is such a good idea.

I'm dripping with sweat when I feel the coldness hit me. I look over my shoulder and see Declan standing there with a bottle of cold water. He squeezes the bottle and shoots me with another round of cold water before I laugh.

"You have to know that feels extremely good right now," I tease him. That cocky grin on his face is too goddamn perfect.

"Figured that much. You done?"

He nods toward the equipment before I say, "Yeah. I need to get over to the club, though." I turn and walk away from him, remembering I'm still pissed off at him. His smile may have dazzled me for a second, but reality caught up real quick. He left me alone in that hotel room that night after our talk. By the time I woke up the next morning he was already waiting outside ready to leave. We haven't talked in weeks, and it's a weight bearing down on me.

"Where the hell do you think you're going?" I hear Charles' voice. I turn to see him stopping Declan as I walk into the girl's locker room.

"I need to talk to my girl," Declan says, his face changing from charming to deadly in seconds. Shit! He can't do that in here.

"It's ok, Charles. He's with me. I was just going to change, and we'll get out of here."

Charles looks over his shoulder at me and shakes his head. "I hope you know what you're doing, Brooke. Your daddy would roll over in his grave," he says before walking away.

My heart races at his words. He's right, though. My dad was against everything Declan believes in; he was the complete opposite.

"Asshole," Declan grumbles, stepping closer to me.

"He's not. He's a good guy. He's just watching out for me." I look at him as I wipe the sweat from my neck with my towel. "What is it you wanted?"

Dec's eyes move over me, and my body heats from the inside out. I want nothing more than to have him fuck me senseless but I won't. He walked away from me.

"We need to talk," he says finally meeting my gaze.

"We are."

"Don't be a smartass, Brooke."

"Declan. It's been weeks. I get it, ok? You changed your mind. It's fine. I'm fine. I have work to do." I start to turn when he grabs my arm. He yanks me toward him roughly.

"We're not done," he growls in my ear.

"Do you realize that you are the criminal in a gym that associates with cops?" I grit my teeth as he squeezes my arm tightly. I can't help it, I'm pissed.

"Is that why you're here? Daddy keep you in check with them?" he growls.

My heart sinks. All the color leaves my face. He knows. He knows my dad was a cop. That wasn't something I wanted him to know. I didn't want him to look at me differently, but now he knows.

"No. I always felt safe here. I had a connection to him here." I shake my arm free of his grasp and hurry into the locker room, rushing to get away from him. I shower quickly and change, hoping like hell that he left. I can't do this with him today. I don't want to. I have too much going on at the club to fight with him about this.

I peek around the corner of the locker room trying to check if he's still here or not. Charles' laughing catches my attention.

"He left, honey," he says when he sees me looking. I smile before I step out. "He bothering you, Brooke?" he asks, his tone changing in seconds.

"No, he's a friend, Charles. We just haven't been getting along lately," I tell him as I set my bag on the counter.

"I could see that. Is he a good friend of yours?" I know what he's asking me. I know that he wants to know and that it's only for my wellbeing.

"He is. He was helping me with some things at the club. We just had a disagreement is all."

Charles nods his head before he says, "If you need anything, you call me."

I nod with a smile before grabbing my bag and head outside. Once outside, I have the shit scared out of me, caught off guard by his words. I was so lost in thoughts I didn't see him or his bike.

"It's cute how you thought we were done talkin'."

"Jesus Christ!" I scream with my hands up, ready to fight. When I see it's him I lower them.

"Why the fuck are you still here?" I ask him, annoyed as hell. I thought the dick left.

"I told you we weren't done talkin'. Get on," he says, nodding toward his bike. I shake my head and start to walk away. His hand grabs mine, and the fire that races through me is unsettling.

"Why are you doing this, Declan?" I ask, letting my head drop. I can't handle this. I can't handle the unsure Declan anymore.

"I fucked up when I claimed you the way I did. I didn't want you in my world like that. I don't want you to be a target and get hurt, Brooke."

Oh, that was fucking comforting! I jerk my arm trying to get away from him.

"I'm so fucking sorry you messed up! Don't worry though; we are nothing, Declan!" I snap. In response, his eyes flash with anger before he yanks my body into his.

"Oh, butterfly. You don't get it, do you? I said I fucked up when I claimed you the way I did, not that I claimed you. Whatever the fuck you have rollin' around in that head of yours, get it the fuck out now. You are mine. Nothin' is changin' that. Now get that sexy ass on the back of my bike."

His hand slams against my ass, making me yelp from the sting. I walk over, sling my bag across my body so I can climb on his bike, and wait. He grins like a fucking lunatic. If he wasn't so fucking sexy, I'd slap the shit out of him. With that look in his eyes though, all I want to do is climb up his big hard body and ride him.

Chapter 33

Declan

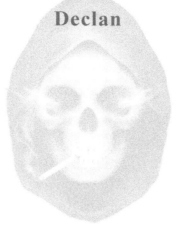

I let her get some work done. I know she needed to. She doesn't pay attention to me; she's got her head in the paperwork in front of her. I take a moment to lean back with my boots kicked up on the desk and watch her. Her hair falls around her face, framing it. The little crease in between her eyes tells me she's focusing on the task at hand. She makes even paperwork look sexy as fuck. I don't say a word, but when she starts chewing on the end of her pen, I about lose it. With a growl, I adjust my dick and say, "You're gonna have to stop doin' that."

Brooke looks up at me before she smiles.

"I'm not doing anything. Why are you still here?" she snaps, the smile leaving her face. I hate that she's pissed off. I hate that there is nothing I can do about it, either. I know that I need to ask her some more questions, but I can't seem to wrap my head around how to do that.

"So, your dad was a cop," I say. Just blurt it out there. That's one way to do it. We might as well get this over with now.

"Yep."

"How long?" I ask. She doesn't look like she wants to talk about this. Too fucking bad.

"His whole life. Since he was nineteen." She looks back at the papers in front of her trying to avoid my gaze.

"You didn't think that was important information to share with me?" I ask. Her eyes come to meet mine, and I can see the loss and hurt in them.

"No, I didn't. That has nothing to do with us."

I huff when those words leave her mouth. Nothing to do with us? That's a fucking good one.

"That right?" I ask her before I lean forward and rest my elbows on my knees. "You work out at the cop's gym. You have a secret code with a curtain. You're fuckin' a criminal, and you didn't

182

think that had anything to do with us?" I ask. My anger is boiling inside of me. She's pushing my buttons, and she knows it.

"Do I associate with cops? Only at the gym. I don't know many of them anymore. Do I have a secret routine I use with Ashley? Yes, I do. And as far as I can remember that criminal fucking left me in a hotel room and I haven't seen him in weeks. So, to answer your question, no, Declan I didn't think that information was important," she throws back at me.

She slams her pen on the desk before shoving out of her chair. She starts for the door, but I stop her.

"You're makin' this harder than it needs to be." I stand up and turn to face her. She spins around, pinning me in place with that glare.

"I am? You walked away, Declan. I took the hint! I'm not a stupid person!" she yells. I watch the fire inside of her erupt like a volcano. She's a fucking burning inferno, and I want nothing more than to touch her flames. I let a smile creep across my face while she watches me.

"Do you know the first time I knew you were special?" I ask her, changing the subject altogether.

"No," she snaps. Look at her. Trying to hold on to her anger but she wants to know. She wants me to tell her all about it.

"You walked up to my clubhouse gate and demanded one of my prospects give you a beer." She brings her gorgeous eyes to meet mine, and there she is. The girl who stole my fucking heart. The one who holds it in her palms and doesn't even know it yet. I take a step toward her, my heart beating wildly in my chest.

"I walked you home, and I fucked you against your friend's house with my gun. You didn't know me then. Why'd you let me do it?" I ask her. I lift my hand and wrap it around the back of her neck, pulling her closer to me. Her hands land on my chest, holding herself up.

"You felt safe. I didn't know how to explain then, and I still don't. You felt like a safe place for me." A single tear slides down her cheek. It's my tear. She's giving it to me, and I'm going to take it. I press my lips to the wet streak on her cheek before I look at her.

"And now?"

"You feel like home, Declan." She cries harder now. I pull her into my chest and hold her tightly.

"That's because you are mine, Brooke. This is home. Right here inside me. This is you." I grab her hand and rest it on my chest. Her tears fall harder and faster, but I don't let her go. I'm done fighting this thing between us. I'm done letting the outside world rule over what we have. I know in my heart that she's all I need, and I will do whatever it takes to keep her there.

"I'm sorry, Declan," she cries, fisting my shirt in her hands.

"No, baby. I am. I shouldn't have pushed you. I shouldn't have let things get out of hand." Before I can finish what I was saying, the sounds of shattering glass explode around us. Brooke jolts but doesn't scream. That's my girl!

"What the hell is happening?" She looks up at me with wide eyes.

"Stay down and stay close to me," I tell her. I pull out my phone and call Blu.

"Yo, Declan."

"We got shots bein' fired down at Leggs."

"Be there in ten." The line goes dead.

"Guys are comin'. Look at me, Brooke." When she brings her eyes to meet mine, I see it for the first time. Fear.

"I won't let anyone hurt you. You trust me?" I ask her. She nods her head as I smile.

"Good girl. Stay behind me," I warn her.

Chapter 34
Brooke

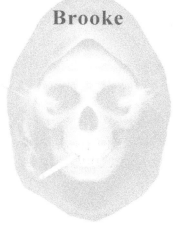

It sounds like fucking explosions going off. I hang onto the back of Declan's shirt like I was told to do. We creep down the hallway toward the back door. There's a strange feeling in the pit of my stomach. I don't like it.

"Oh, Brookey!" I hear my name being called, but Declan keeps us moving. He turns quickly when he hears something behind us. His gun is trained on the man standing at the end of the hallway that I didn't even hear come up.

"You picked the wrong club, asshole," Declan growls. The man smiles while Dec pushes me farther behind him.

"No, this is our club," the guy says. I can see his finger nearing the trigger. My heart starts to race as I gasp. Dec fires, the man falling to the floor and before I can register anything else, Declan spins us around, pushing me behind him in one swift move.

The back door had opened at some point, and a man is firing at us. Declan pulls the trigger on his own gun but instantly falls back, crushing me to the ground.

It all happened in slow motion. The ringing in my ears is so loud. My eyes flutter from hitting my head on the floor. A wave of nausea overwhelms me. I can faintly hear screaming around me, but every time I blink my eyes, I see spots.

"Brooke!" It's Declan's voice that snaps me out of whatever fog I'm in. He hovers over me. The lights are blinding.

"You're ok, baby," he says. I nod, but I feel sick. I turn my head and heave, but nothing comes out. I'm scooped into Declan's arms before he passes me off to someone else.

"Get her back to the clubhouse. Lock it the fuck down!" Declan roars. I can feel myself being carried out of the club. The night air hits me and a new wave of nausea hits.

"I'm going to be sick," I grumble under my breath.

"It's ok, darlin'. I've been puked on before." The chuckle comes out of his mouth before I realize it's Mayhem.

"Where's Dec?" I ask as a new wave of panic sneaking its way in.

"He'll meet us at the clubhouse. Let's get you back and let Doc check you out."

My eyes flutter shut again. I can feel myself being put into the back of a car, but that's about it. I can't open my eyes. My head pounds. The ringing in my ears is almost too much to handle. I can feel the car moving and vaguely hear Mayhem rambling on about something, but my head is swimming. I keep my eyes closed tightly thinking that may help hold the nausea in.

"Mayhem?" I ask out loud. Or I think I did.

"Yeah, sweetheart?"

"Am I dead?" I don't know why I asked. I feel dead. Maybe I am.

Mayhem chuckles before he says, "No, you ain't dead and don't go dyin' on me on the way back either. Dec will kill me, and then you'll be stuck in the ghost world with me." His words aren't very reassuring. In fact, they are downright scary.

Would Declan kill for me? I have no doubt in my mind that he would. He promised to take care of me and protect me. Why would I think he wouldn't kill for me, too?

Chapter 35
Declan

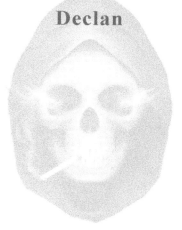

"Come on, brother. Let him stitch it up!" Tic says, shoving me back onto the bed.

"Fuck off, Tic. I need to see her," I say as I try to shove myself back up.

"She's fine. I took care of her. She's probably asleep anyway. She's got a concussion from hell," Doc says.

I relax a little knowing that she's going to be ok. I just want to see her. Touch her. Know that she's ok. I need to see it with my own eyes.

"Went straight through," Doc says as he stitches my arm up. I already knew that. The adrenaline racing through my body right now will surely wear off and remind me of how bad it hurts later.

"You sure she don't need to go to the ER?" I ask Doc, watching him place the needle through my skin.

"No. I think she's ok, Declan," he reminds me again. I close my eyes as Doc continues to stitch my arm up.

When he's done, he says, "I'd tell you to keep it clean and all that shit, but you won't listen." He shoves off his chair and heads toward the door.

"Thanks, Doc."

Blu walks in eyeing me. "You good?" I nod once before he sits in the chair. "This shit got too close to home, brother," he says. I agree there.

"You get a good look?" I ask. Blu nods before he leans forward, resting his arms on his knees.

"It's Dragons. The one you shot is dead. So are a few others. They were all wearin' those goddamn Dragons colors." Blu huffs out a breath.

"What do we do now?" I ask, ready to take on the goddamn world. They shot at my girl. My fucking girl! That shit isn't going to be left alone until I kill the motherfuckers.

"Got Mystic checkin' security. Seein' which way they went. Prospects are out searchin' the streets to see if they are lingerin' around anywhere. Mayhem went out with Bones to check on the warehouses. This doesn't look like it was comin' at us," he says, blowing out a breath.

If they weren't coming for us, then they were coming for her.

"They wanted Brooke," I say, already knowing the truth. I shove off the bed and walk toward the door when Blu stops me.

"We're goin' after them. We just need a set plan. She's family, Dec. We protect family."

I glance over my shoulder and give him a quick nod. He's right. She is family, and I'm about to go remind her of that.

The walk down the hall is a blur. That shit happened so quickly I barely had time to react. I hate that I hurt her too, but that wasn't really my fault. That blast sent my ass flying. I open the door to my room and find her sitting up in bed with something in her hand.

"How you feelin'?" She looks up at me with tears in her beautiful eyes.

"I'm ok. You're bleeding," she gasps, throwing the sheets back. I stop her, putting my hand up.

"Don't get up. You've got a concussion from hell from what Doc said." She nods, and I can see just how unsteady she is. "Lay back down, butterfly."

"He was killed when I was seven. The guy that killed him wasn't even a guy. He was a kid," she says softly. Jesus Christ. Here she goes. She's giving me her past. She's giving me a piece of herself right now.

"How did you find out?" I ask her while I move toward the chair next to the bed.

"I was there. So was Angel." My heart kicks up a notch. There's no fucking way in hell.

"Where were you?" I ask swallowing hard. This can't be happening.

"We were outside in front of the house."

My stomach drops. I'm fucked. Bile races up my throat. I swallow hard, willing it all to stay down.

"You don't need to talk right now," I tell her not wanting her to keep going. This is it. The end of my fucking world is about to spill from those lips.

"I need to. We were out there welcoming him home from work. It was late, but Uncle Devon let us stay up just that once. Angel and I ran out the door as soon as we saw the headlights. He was crossing the street, and we ran and leaped into his arms. He was hugging us tightly when someone walked up to us."

I run my hand over my face. Son of a bitch!

"Brooke." I want her to stop. I can't handle it. I'm the motherfucker who broke her. I'm the one who took that life away from her. Fuck.

"The kid shot him, Dec. Right in front of me! What kind of monster does that?" she cries.

Me. I'm that monster. I'm the kind of monster that could take a life and walk away like it was nothing. I'm the one!

"The boy. He was only a boy. He didn't want to do it. I could see it in his eyes. They made him do it. When they all walked off, he leaned down to me. He gave me-" she cries, but I don't let her finish.

I finish the sentence for her. "A rosary."

Chapter 36

Brooke

There are tears in his eyes. I've never seen a single tear come close to Declan's eyes, but there they are.

"What did you say?" I ask, shifting in the bed.

"A rosary. He gave you a rosary. He told you it would keep you safe." His voice is low and strangled.

How did he know that? How could he have known? I never told anyone about that, not even Angel.

"How do you know that, Declan?"

His eyes fall on my hands. The rosary sits in my palm, my fingers gently caressing the cross like I've always done when I'm scared.

"I'm that boy, Brooke," he says softly, his voice dancing with emotions.

"No. You weren't," I retort. There's no way it was Dec.

I watch him swallow hard, sniffing back the tears before he says, "My dad was president at the time. He wanted me to join the club, prove myself loyal to them. I wanted that, too. It was my life. Your dad killed my mom, Brooke."

I gasp at his words. I shake my head. My dad never had to kill anyone. He told me that himself.

"No! He said he never killed anyone, that he was lucky enough to never have to kill anyone!" I scream. That can't be true. There's no way that can be true. But when I look up and meet the tear-filled eyes of Declan, I know in my heart that it is.

"Why? Why would he kill her?" I ask, a sobbing mess. I feel like I'm coming apart at the seams.

"We were walkin' home from the store one night. He saw the cut she had on. He knew who she was. Your dad was a dirty cop, Brooke. He killed her just for bein' married to my dad. For bein' a part of this club!" Declan roars as tears fall down his face. "I was doin' what was right! An eye for an eye!" He screams louder.

The door cracks open, interrupting any further words from Declan. Mayhem step in, more somber than I've ever seen him.

"Blu needs you," he says quietly to Dec.

I watch Declan wipe his eyes before turning to his brother. "Keep an eye on her." He nods toward me.

"Go to hell, Declan! I hate you! I will never forgive you for what you did! Never!" I scream as hot tears fall down my cheeks.

Declan watches me as I fall apart in front of his eyes.

"I love you, butterfly. That doesn't change."

He turns and quickly walks out, leaving me to my mess of tears and a spinning head. Mayhem drops in the chair but doesn't say a word. I don't want him to. I don't want to be here.

"I want to go home," I say.

"Not happenin'," Mayhem responds quickly.

"Why?" I look over at him, and he shrugs.

"Someone's tryin' to kill you. You're safe here. We will protect you." The words leave his mouth, but all I can think about is what Declan said.

"Who's going to protect Declan?"

His eyebrows furrow as he looks at me. He leans closer to me before he asks, "Why would Declan need protection?"

"He killed my father. I'm going to kill him." My voice is as strong as I've ever heard it. There is so much hatred inside of me. Hatred toward Declan for what he said. Hatred toward my dad for lying to me. Hatred toward everyone who knew and let me suffer all these years, wondering why my dad left us too soon.

"I don't know what he did or didn't do, but he loves you, darlin'. You won't kill him," Mayhem says with confidence.

"I won't? Are you sure about that?"

Mayhem raises his eyebrows at me, pondering my statement. The words are ringing loud and clear in his head.

"You say he killed your dad?" he asks. I nod.

"Long time ago, wasn't it?"

"I was seven," I snap.

"He tell you why he did it?" Mayhem asks, eyeing me the whole time. He knows too, doesn't he?

"Yeah. He said my dad was a dirty cop and that he killed his mom." Mayhem nods his head before pulling his phone out of his pocket.

"Yo, Mystic. Need a favor, brother." I hear him talking into the phone.

"Get me the information on an old file. Sheriff Charleston. Killed outside his home a few blocks down."

"Yeah, that'd be the one. Send it up with Mouse to Declan's room."

Mayhem crosses his arms over his chest as he glares at me.

"My uncle was a piece of shit president. Even worse of a father. He put his son in more compromisin' positions than I can count. Declan couldn't get out of them - it's the club's way of life. You think he wanted to kill your dad? You are dead fuckin' wrong. He may have felt that urge because of what your dad did to his mom, but I promise you that was a forced kill. Declan knew

201

his place from day one. He was raised here." A knock on the door stops him from talking.

"Open it!" he hollers over his shoulder. Mouse walks in with a thick file in his hand.

"Here you go, Mayhem." He grabs the file and nods toward Mouse. Mayhem stands up and tosses the file on my lap.

"Look at it. Your dad was as dirty as they come. He wasn't in our pocket darlin', but he was in someone's. Take a look for yourself before you shovel shit at Dec," he snaps. He turns away from me and walks to the corner. He presses his hands against the wall and lets his head fall forward.

"Why are you doing this?" I whisper.

He doesn't turn to look at me, but he says, "'Cause Dec isn't just my cousin. He's my brother by every meanin' of the word. He's my family. I've never seen the motherfucker as happy as I have since you been around. You want to ruin him? You need all the fuckin' information before you can pass that kind of judgement. Once you have it all, you can decide if that's really the way you want to handle this."

Chapter 37

Declan

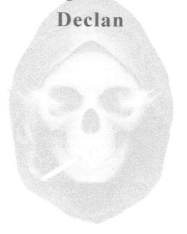

My head's a goddamn mess. I can't think straight. I want to throw up. I want to punch a fucking wall. I want to run. None of those are options, though. I walk into Blu's office and drop into the chair.

"What the fuck's wrong with you?" he asks.

I lift my head and look at the man who took my father's place. The one who ran this club the way it should have been run. The man who has been more of a father to me than mine ever was.

"You remember back when I was fifteen and dad made me kill that cop for killin' mom?" Blu's face scrunches as he tries to remember back to that time.

"The one down the road? What about it?" he asks.

I know it was so fucking long ago that I shouldn't even be talking about it. But the past has a way of catching up with you. Mine just caught up with me.

"That cop was Brooke's dad. She was the fuckin' little girl on the goddamn ground cryin'."

Blu's eyes widen before he blows out a breath. "You sure?"

"She's sittin' in my goddamn room right now with the rosary my mom gave me. The one I gave her that night." I run my hand through my hair waiting on Blu to process what the hell I just said. He looks as lost as I feel.

"She knows it was you now?"

I give him a nod before I pull out a cigarette and light it up. I blow out a ring of smoke before I pull my eyes to Blu's. "She hates me now, brother. She doesn't wanna be here. She wants out. As soon as we handle the Dragons, I'm lettin' her go." It breaks me down inside to even say that. It kills a part of me to know that I have to let her go.

"You sure about that?" Blu crosses his arms over his chest and gazes at me.

"Yeah. She doesn't want that life with me. I can't fuckin' blame her. I killed her fuckin' dad, man."

Blu nods but doesn't say anything else. A knock on the door pulls Blu's attention. "Yeah!" he hollers.

"Yo, Declan. You might wanna go see what the fuck is goin' on in your room brother. It sounds like a goddamn tornado is blowin' through there." Mouse looks pretty damn amused by all of this.

"Fuck!" I grumble, passing him the cigarette before heading out of the office. As soon as my feet hit the damn floor, I can hear her screaming. It's not a fear cry, either. No, this is worse. She's fucking pissed. I rush down the hall and shove the door open to find her tearing my room to hell and back. Mayhem stands off to the side, his arms crossed over his chest, a cigarette hanging from his lips. He looks as calm and collected as always. He meets my gaze before nodding to the file on the bed.

"What the fuck did you do?" I ask him. Why the fuck would he have shown her the files we had on her dad? What the hell was he thinking!

"Showed her the truth, brother."

I walk toward the bed and pick up a few of the photos. Is that her mom? Jesus Christ! Was he involved in her mom's death? I flip through a few more pages and find that my assumption was right.

"Fuck!" I roar. I look over my shoulder, but Mayhem isn't there. Sneaky fucker. I look up at Brooke as she stares at her hands, her little fit finally coming to an end.

"Did you know?" she asks, her voice hoarse from screaming.

"About your mom? No, I didn't." She looks up, her face red and puffy from crying and screaming. It kills me. It rips pieces of my heart out to see her hurting like this.

"He had her killed, Declan. Why? What kind of man would do that?" she asks me. She watches me intently, waiting for me to give her an answer that I don't have.

"I don't know, Brooke. I'm sorry." She just looks at me, not moving. My heart hammers in my chest.

Brooke's eyes leave mine and dart around the room. She drops to her knees quickly and starts picking up the mess she made. She's lost. She doesn't know what to do with herself. Everything she was ever told was a lie. They all lied to her.

"Brooke," I say her name softly. She doesn't look up. Her hands keep moving, picking up the mess.

"Brooke," I say her name a little firmer this time. She drops the broken beer bottle that was in her hand. Her eyes come to meet mine.

"Come here." She shakes her head slowly, not sure what to do.

"Brooke, come here," I say once more. I watch her slowly shove herself off the floor. She takes slow steps toward me like a scared kitten. I watch her lip quiver before I grab her and pull her into me.

She unleashes all the anger, hurt, and rage she feels. The betrayal. Her body shakes and shudders with each breath she takes. Each one kills another piece of me. I wish I could take her pain away, but instead I caused her pain, too.

"I'm so sorry, Brooke. You have no idea how much."

Chapter 38

Brooke

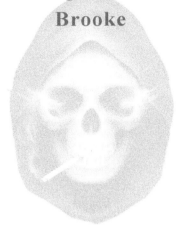

Dec sat with me, rubbing my hair away from my face as I cried into his shirt. He never said a word. He only held me tight, knowing that's exactly what I needed. I fell asleep at some point. I don't know when he left, but I woke up alone and the bed is cold. I pull the blankets off my body before standing. I made the biggest mess in here, and I feel like shit for it.

"What the hell is wrong with you, Brooke?" I ask myself.

I start to collect the trash and papers I flung everywhere when I see her picture. I pick it up and hold it in my hands. My mom. She was beautiful. I don't remember much about her. She was killed in a car accident right after Angel was born. I run my fingers over her image. I miss my life. I miss the life I had once before, the life I thought I had. It's all gone now. All I have left is Angel.

"Liar. You have Dec," I mumble to myself. He's right. I do have him. He's been there for me when I needed him. He's told me he loved me. as hard as that is to accept. He might have killed my dad, but my dad was dirty. He was dirtier than any of us ever knew.

I drop the photo onto the floor and stand up. I head out into the hallway determined to apologize to Dec. When I step into the main room, it's eerily silent. I glance around and only see some of the club girls.

"Cherry!" I call out to her when I notice her across the room.

She turns to look at me, her hair draping over her shoulder. She gives me that giant grin of hers before she says, "Brooke! I didn't realize you were here." She comes bounding toward me, her smile getting bigger.

"Do you know where Declan is?" I ask her. She shakes her head.

"No, I just got here. The bikes are gone, though." My heart starts beating faster.

I glance around until I see Mouse. I head straight toward him.

"Mouse, where's Dec?" I ask. He smiles at me.

"Can't tell you that, darlin'."

I know it's all club rules and bullshit. I've heard it over and over again. I watch his face, and I can already tell he isn't going to give me the answers I want. Tough shit. I want answers, and he's going to give them to me. I reach up and grab him around the neck in a choke-style hold.

"I want to know where the fuck Declan is now!" I roar. Mouse tries to fight me, but I don't let him go. He grabs me around the waist, pulling me, but I rotate my body and keep my hold tight.

"Where is he?" I yell. The girls have gathered around to watch what I'm doing.

Mouse gasps, fighting for air. All he has to do is tell me what I want to know.

"He's on a run! The Dragons. They were after you!" he hisses out.

I loosen my grip when Cherry yells, "Tap out!" I want to laugh, but I'm serious. I want to know where Declan is.

"Where?"

"I don't know!" I let him go as he drops to his knees, catching his breath.

Glancing around, I feel like I'm in a panic. I want to go after him. I want to tell him that I love him too. I want him to hold me and tell me that everything is ok.

"I have to go," I say out loud, but more to myself. Mouse jumps up off the floor and comes at me quickly.

"You can't! I have orders." I glare at him as he gets closer to me.

"I'll kick your ass, Mouse. What's worse? Them or me? The embarrassment that a girl kicked your ass or Declan?" I tempt him. I don't want to hurt Mouse, but I will. If he doesn't leave me alone, I will.

"Goddamn you, Brooke!" he roars and steps to the side. I knew I'd get my way.

I rush out the door but have no clue where to go. I don't know anything about this MC shit. I don't know where they hang out or what they do. I almost feel defeated. If they were looking for me, then they would know I'm always at the club. I run down the street and grab my car, heading to Leggs.

As I drive, things run through my head. I don't want to lose Declan. He's been the one solid thing that I've had in a long time. I pull my cell out and call Angel to make sure she's ok.

"Hey, sis," she says happily into the phone. I smile from just hearing her voice.

"Hey, Angel. You doing ok?" I ask as I speed down the road.

"I'm good. This school is amazing. You have to come visit."

I knew her going to college would be the best thing for her. She deserves to live her life. She deserves to have everything she's ever wanted in life.

"I will soon. I'm heading to the club. I just wanted to tell you I love you." *In case I don't get a second chance to do it*. I leave the last part unsaid.

Chapter 39

Declan

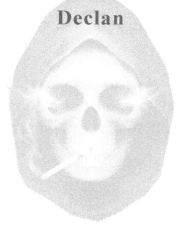

"This is bullshit." I blow out a cloud of smoke. I glance around the empty bar beginning to get a little pissed off. We chose this bar since it was neutral territory.

"You don't think they'll show?" Blu asks looking over the room.

"Why the fuck would they?" I ask.

When Blu put a call into the Dragons President, he wanted to meet immediately. He claims that he doesn't know anything about the attacks at the club. He said that he had a few guys go rogue, but I don't believe that shit for a second. How the fuck would a president not know what the hell his own guys were doing?

"Wanna drink?" Mayhem leans over the counter and grabs a bottle of Jack.

I watch him take the lid off and drink straight from the bottle.

"Nice cup." I chuckle. He nods his head before passing me the bottle. As I take a long pull, I hear the rumble of the engines.

"Here we go," I say.

Blu steps toward the door with me and Tic close behind. My hand's on my gun, ready to fire, and take out anyone that might have shot at my girl. We step outside the door and onto the dusty pavement. I take in the Dragon's as they stand there behind their president, ready for anything. I don't miss their wandering gazes more than likely thinking the same about us.

"You Blu?" The main man asks as he climbs off his bike. Blu watches him intently as he steps closer. All of us are on edge as we take in the other club. As calm as it seems right now, that can change in an instant.

"I'm Blu."

"I'm Nixon. You wanna tell me why the fuck you think we had shit to do with your club?" The man is clearly pissed by the accusations.

"Your men were found dead or did you not fuckin' notice?" I throw back at him as I step up next to Blu. My hands clench at my sides, but what I really want is to blow his damn head off.

"We don't have any missin' men! Why the fuck you think we're here?" he snaps, his nostrils flaring.

"They had on Dragon cuts!" I retort.

"You tellin' me I don't know my own men? You're askin' for war." He grits his teeth. I take a step forward when Blu steps in front of me.

"We had three dead in the motherfuckin' club. All three had Dragons cuts on! Why don't you tell me what that means?" Blu growls. He advances on the guy; his rage is palpable.

"You have my fuckin' word that those weren't my men. You think I'm a fuckin' coward? I'd stake claim to anything that I did!"

I watch the look in his eyes. He's not lying no matter how much I wanted to think he was. Someone used his club as a front and Brooke is in danger. I need to know she's okay right now.

"Fuck!" I roar, pulling my cell phone from my pocket. I dial Mouse.

"Hey, Dec. I tried to keep her here. She fuckin' choked me, brother."

I don't even let him finish talking. I hit the end button and yell as loud as my lungs will let me. If anything happens to her, I swear to God, I will take everyone out.

"What's the problem?" Blu turns on his heel to look at me.

"She's gone. Kicked Mouse's ass and left."

The guys all curse under their breath when Nixon speaks. "I got a spot right down the road. You wanna hit it? Get my boys runnin' some intel?"

Blu's eyes come to meet mine. I nod once. "We won't say sorry; it's not how we roll. We fuckin' saw the cuts and went with it," I tell Nixon.

He shakes his head clearly understanding what I'm saying. "No worries on that, brother. I would have done the same. Let's find your girl and the motherfuckers usin' my club." I can see it in his eyes - he's ok with this.

"Let's roll!" I bellow out.

I climb on my bike and rev the engine. The need to get the fuck out of here and find my girl is eating at me. The not knowing where she is is what's killing me. I hate that sense of dread tugging at my gut. I hate that I can't be there holding her, protecting her, like I promised.

We pull out and follow behind the Dragons. I don't know where the fuck they are taking us, but I want to believe that they are telling the truth. Nothing in his posture or tone makes me believe otherwise.

I get lost in the rhythm of the road as we ride. My head is spinning. There are so many things I want to say to her. So, many things I want to share with her. I don't want to miss my chance because something has happened to her. I fucking love that girl, and when I get my hands on her, I'm never letting her go.

Chapter 40

Brooke

I park the car and head into the back door of the club. I know it isn't open. Hell, I'm the one who closed it down after that shoot out. Declan told me the guys took care of the dead bodies that littered my floor. I didn't ask questions simply because I didn't want to know the answers.

I step through the door and around all the plaster that was crumbled by the gunfire. I shake my head knowing that I may never get the chance to open this club back up and get it running. My uncle would be so disappointed in me for letting all this come down. He worked harder than anyone I know to keep this club going, and I ruined it.

Heading into my office, I sit in my chair and think. If they aren't here where the fuck are they? I can't let Declan get hurt for something that doesn't have to do with his club. He's too much of a good person. Sure, he does illegal things, but he's good to me.

I lay my head on the desk until I hear a noise. I slip off the chair and slowly creep around the desk and toward the door.

I start to look out when big hands grab me. My instincts kick in. My training flashes before my eyes. I throw the first punch, colliding with a bone. When I'm grabbed from behind, I throw my head back before I hear it.

"Jesus Christ, butterfly."

My heart starts thudding in my ears. I look over my shoulder and collapse into Declan's arms.

"Oh my God, Declan! You scared the shit out of me!" I yell at him. He holds me tighter, a chuckle vibrating through his chest.

"Sorry. You wanna tell me how you got away from Mouse?" When he sets me down, I turn to face him and take in his disapproving expression.

"I might have threatened him," I say sheepishly.

"You might have threatened one of my prospects? Is that what you're tellin' me?" His face remains stern. My heart kicks up a notch.

"Yeah. I might have headlocked him, too." I look away not wanting to meet his gaze any longer than I have to. His hand comes up to cup my cheek, pulling my face back to his.

"So, you think you can just threaten my prospects and headlock them and run the fuck away from me? Is that what you're doin'?" His eyes burn into me. So, deeply.

"Declan, I just wanted to find you."

His lips slam into mine. His tongue darts into my mouth. The way he kisses me makes my heart stop. The world around us stops.

"You can't do that without payin' for it," Declan growls. He holds me close, the world slowly coming back into view.

"I think you're both gonna be payin'."

A growl startles me from behind. Declan's eyes go wide. His features harden.

"You the motherfucker that came after my girl?" The growl that leaves him rattles me through his chest.

"You made it easy," the guy says.

I turn in Declan's arms and gasp. My mind works overtime trying to put a name to this face. I know this man! I've seen him before.

"Who the fuck are you?" Declan asks.

The guy grins, his gun trained on us. "She's figurin' it out." He nods at me. Declan pulls me closer to him.

"I'm gonna ask you again. Who the fuck are you?" Declan gets louder this time. He's vibrating behind me. His rage is off the charts. I can feel it.

"Uncle Darren?" I say not sure that I remember him exactly. As soon as his smile reaches his eyes, I know it's him. He looks just a lot like my dad. I haven't seen him in years, not since I was a kid. He came to my dad's funeral but disappeared after that.

"Now you remember me," Darren says.

"Why? Why are you doing this?" I ask. Declan's hands clench around my waist.

"Oh, come on, Brooke! Your dad and uncle had it all. This club was supposed to be mine!" he roars.

"Nothing was yours! My uncle worked hard for this club, and my dad was a fucking coward. Just like you!" At my words, Darren takes a step toward me, but Declan throws me behind him.

"Don't you fuckin' talk to me like that!" Darren roars.

"You bastard!" I scream. I try to go after him, but Declan holds me back.

"You got two choices here, Darren. Take a fuckin' walk, or you're dead," Declan growls from behind me.

"I don't think that's right," another voice booms from behind us.

Chapter 41

Declan

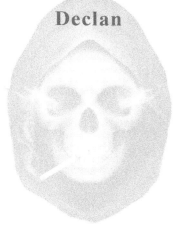

My body is a bundle of energy. My nerves are firing off. I want to strangle that motherfucker with my bare hands. I want to watch him bleed for what he's done to Brooke.

"You motherfuckers are makin' a big fuckin' mistake here," I give them a warning.

"We want what belongs to us," Darren sneers.

I can feel the presence of the other guy behind us. I don't need to look at the motherfucker to know he's there. Luckily, the guys will be headed here soon too. I knew something was off. I could feel it. I opted to come here rather than to go with them to collect the intel. I knew there was something more to this place. All I have to do is stall them until my boys show up.

"You killed him, didn't you?" Brooke asks, moving around to my side. I let her. I don't trust the motherfuckers in this room to not shoot her when she isn't looking.

"He was in the way, Brooke. I tried to reason it out with him. Tried talking to him. He didn't want to. I had to make him understand that I meant business. Then I found out he was leaving it all to you."

I swallow hard listening to the story coming out of his mouth. I want to shove my fist through his face.

"You were a coward! Why couldn't you make your own way!" she accuses as tears fall down her cheeks.

"You were never a threat, Brooke. I could have killed you. I could have muscled you into what I wanted, but then you went and got mixed up with this idiot." Darren nods toward me.

Brooke starts to move, her body coiling with anger. I grip her around the waist, pulling her back into me.

"When I say 'now', you jump into that room. Got it?" I whisper in her ear, appearing to calm her.

Brooke starts to shake her head when I squeeze her a little tighter. I give her enough warning.

"That's enough of this shit. Now!" I roar. I shove Brooke toward the door to her office, reaching for my gun with the other hand. I fire a shot at Darren before ducking and firing at the idiot behind me. I feel the sting as it rips through my chest. One of the assholes got a shot off, but I took the other fucker down.

I drop to the ground and roll onto my back, my gun still in hand. That's when I see Darren holding his shoulder standing over me.

"We seem to have a situation now," he says with an evil grin on his face. His gun's aimed at my head, but I'm barely holding onto mine with the pain shooting through my chest. I let my arm fall to the side, the gun hitting the floor as I look up at him breathlessly.

"Do it, you fuckin' coward," I growl at him. He takes a step toward me, leaning down closer.

"You weren't shit to begin with. You were nothing to anyone. You couldn't take care of her," he says in a low gruff tone.

"I can take care of myself," Brooke says. The sound of a gunshot rocks the room but the blood seeping from his head before he falls on top of me is what makes me smile. His body falls roughly onto me before Brooke screams. I'm pushing him off with one hand while Brooke pulls and rolls him.

"God, Declan!" she cries when she looks down at me.

"I'm ok, butterfly." I shove myself up with one arm trying to catch my breath. I feel like a lead weight has been set on my chest.

"Come here." She reaches down and helps me to my feet. I stumble a little when I notice her face scrunched up.

"What's wrong?" I ask noting the pain in her eyes.

"Nothing. My shoulder is fucked up. Let's get out of here." We lean on each other as we head out the back door.

"You're late!" Brooke yells when she sees the guys climbing off their bikes.

"Yeah. Well, we like to make an entrance." Mayhem grins at her.

"She needs her shoulder checked," I tell him.

"Yeah, 'cause you look great," he comments. I cut my eyes at him when he reaches for Brooke.

"No! Him first. He was shot. I wasn't." Stubborn little ass. I can't wait to get her home and spank her ass.

"Why don't both you motherfuckers get in the truck and let Doc take a look at home. We got this." Blu nods toward the club. I nod my head and walk over to where the truck is.

Nuts sits in the front seat eyeing us as we climb in.

"Next time, you're on guard duty with this one," I tell him nodding to Brooke.

"Sure thing, Dec. I saw how she choked Mouse out, though," he chuckles.

"Take us home."

Chapter 42

Brooke

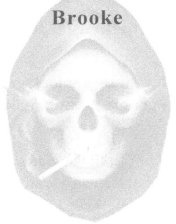

"Stop!" I slap Declan when he tries to get up again. He's really beginning to piss me off. Doc isn't far behind me.

"I don't need to lay here. I can sit," he grumbles.

"Bullet barely missed your damn lung. You lost a lot of blood, Dec, but you'll live," Doc says as he stitches him up.

"Thanks for that update, Doc," he says sarcastically.

"What about her shoulder?" he asks Doc, clearly ignoring the fact that I'm standing here.

"Dislocated. I got it back in place. It'll be sore, but she's fine. Neither of you girls are gonna die today," he says with a laugh.

"I didn't plan on it," I say with a smile. Doc nods and grins at me before getting up.

"Keep the sling on that for a few days at least. Maybe you'll listen better than these men do," Doc mumbles as he leaves the room.

I sit on the edge of the bed in silence. Dec doesn't say anything, and that's part of what's bothering me. I know we left things at an awkward place the other night.

"I'm sorry, Declan." I break the silence. It needs to be said. I need him to know that I'm sorry for doubting him.

"Me too," he says, shoving off the bed. I watch the pain settle across his face. It hurts to see him like this.

"Where are you going?" I ask when he heads toward the door. He stops when his hand lands on the doorknob, but doesn't turn around. My heart thunders in my chest.

"I'm not what you need, Brooke. I always knew you deserved better than me."

I gasp at his words. I don't know what to say to him. I stand here like a fool as I watch Declan slowly walk away. He leaves the door open behind him, which I take as my cue to leave. Big hot tears fall down my cheeks as I run from the room. I turn the corner to head outside when I slam into someone. I look up through the tears and see Tic staring down at me.

"He'll come around," he says softly. Tic and I haven't talked much, but I can tell he's trying to be nice.

"I don't think it's that easy," I tell him. His large hand comes up and wipes the tears from my eyes before grabbing my chin between his fingers.

"Dec's a good guy. He has a huge heart that a lot of women want. Dec doesn't do things halfway. He loves you, Brooke, but he's just a little lost right now. We all get there. Don't give up on him. Come on; I'll walk you home." Tic throws his arm around my waist before leading me out of the clubhouse.

It all feels so surreal. I'm leaving the clubhouse without Declan and going home to nothing.

230

"What are your thoughts on the club?" Tic asks as we walk down the road. I shrug my good shoulder before looking up at him.

"I've worked my ass off trying to keep it going. Now that it's been down for a while and the amount of work that it'll take to get up and running, I don't think I can afford it." It's true. The damage that was done in there was extensive. I was barely keeping it going when my uncle was alive. Now it's just a big mess.

"The construction aspect won't be so bad. My friend owns his own company; I can get him to come in and do it." His words slam into my heart.

We walk for a few minutes in silence until we get to my house. "Why would you do that?"

"You're Dec's old lady, whether you like it or not. He claimed you. You're his. He may be actin' like a dick right now, but he'll come around, Brooke. He needs you, and you need him. We're family."

I stand here staring up at him. We're family. That's what he said, but I don't have anyone anymore.

"Don't doubt us. We're all here, Brooke. I can see the look in your eyes. You might be fightin' with him, but the rest of us are here." He leans down and presses a kiss to my cheek. "Call me if you need anything."

I watch him walk away. I stand here feeling sorry for myself. I don't know what to do with my life, don't know where to turn. I walk inside and the world around me fades. Everything that I've ever wanted has slowly been taken away from me.

Declan hates me. I can't blame him either.

My uncle is dead.

My dad killed my mom.

I can't handle this anymore.

I flop onto the couch and let everything fall away as I cry.

Chapter 43

Declan

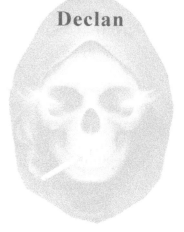

It's been three months since the shit went down with Brooke and her uncle. I couldn't believe how easy it was for him to mimic the fucking Dragons. Once they found the others who Darren was working with, they killed them all. I was ok with that. I was ok letting them take over and handle the rest of them. My heart hasn't been right since she left here, though. It aches for her, but I knew from the day I met her that I wasn't what she needed. She needs and deserves more than I can give her.

"You look like shit," Blu says sitting across from me. I watch him light up a cigarette before passing me one.

"I feel better. This shit won't keep me down." Blu nods as I blow out a ring of smoke.

"I know. We're havin' that party tonight for Cherry's birthday. You still up for it?"

I nod before I say, "Damn right I am. It's been awhile since we had a good one. Nixon and his boys comin' down?"

"Yeah. Now that other shit is sorted out, they're back on good terms with us. That shit could've gone south," he says.

I reach for my beer and take a long pull before I reply. "Yeah. I heard that. Sorry that shit got brought to the club, brother." His eyes meet mine as he shakes his head.

"She's family. Whether you two figure that shit out or not, you claimed her in front of everyone, Dec. We've kept eyes on her. Tic's got his boys over there fixin' the damn club. I put some money in an account to get that shit back up and runnin'. She might not like it, but the club's gonna be a part of that shit. Thought you could talk to her about it." My eyes jerk to his. Has he lost his fucking mind?

"Do you have any idea how pissed she's gonna be that you fronted the money?" I raise my eyebrows. No way in fuck is that information coming from me!

Blu chuckles. "Yeah, I figured she'd be pissed, but it's the only way to get it runnin'. She didn't have the funds to do it, but I know it means a lot to her. Mystic ran her finances and shit."

I nod my head. I know she'd be happy to have it up and running. It may only be a strip club, but it was hers and her uncle's. I know how hard she worked to keep it going for him.

"Maybe Tic can bring it up. They seem to be pretty close these days." I lean back in my chair and blow the smoke from my lungs.

"Tic what?"

I look over my shoulder to see Tic standing there with his arms crossed over his chest.

"You're close with Brooke these days. You can talk to her about the money Blu put into Leggs." I hear him huff, but I turn around not needing to see the look on his face.

"You're pissin' me off, motherfucker," he snaps. I shove out of my chair and glare at him.

"That so? I ain't sayin' shit that ain't true." I can see the anger in his eyes. I don't give a shit either.

"You two wanna calm down?" Blu says, trying to diffuse the situation. It doesn't do anything, though. I know where he's been every fucking day for the last three months.

"Fuck that, Blu. He's in with her; he can talk to her. I got shit to do." I turn and walk away. My heart feels heavy in my chest.

Nothing feels right around here anymore. My attitude has shifted and I take my anger out on my brothers. I don't know what the hell I'm doing anymore. I find myself sitting out back on the picnic table.

"You want some company?" Prim asks. Prim of all people! That girl is as nasty as they come. Her attitude is about as shitty as mine.

"That depends. Are you on the rag? You know you're shitty," I say to her. She gives me a small smile before sitting next to me.

"Why are you so shitty?" I ask her. Me and her have never really talked. She's been around since she was little, but we rarely talk.

"You know what it feels like to love someone you can't have?" I follow her gaze to Blu. I raise my eyebrows. I never realized she had a thing for him.

"What makes you think you can't have him?" She slowly drags her eyes back to me.

"He's in love with someone else. No one sees it but me, but it'll come out eventually," she says with a hint of sadness in her voice.

"You know that for sure?" I ask her. She gives me a small smirk before running a hand through her hair.

"I know that for sure, Declan, or I'd make a move. I may be a club whore, but I'm not a homewrecker. I'd never touch one of the guys who had an old lady or was interested in someone else. I do have some kind of morals," she huffs. I grab her shoulder and pull her into my side.

"You know, I've always watched you walk around here with an attitude. I wondered what the hell pissed you off so badly," I say.

Prim laughs before she says, "Love. This fucked-up heart of mine. Emotions. Hell, what more can I say?" She giggles as she lays her head on my shoulder.

"You'll find the one. It's not your time yet, darlin'," I tell her.

Prim nods before looking up at me. "But it's yours. Don't let her go, Dec. She's a good one. We can all see how happy she makes you. Don't let the little things keep you from the bigger things in life."

Chapter 44

Brooke

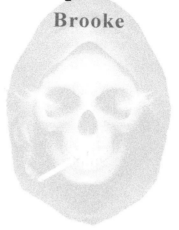

"Ryan!" I yell down the hallway. I'm amazed at the work that Tic and his friends were able to get done in here. Ryan walks in, and I gaze up at him with my puppy dog eyes.

"What? What do you want now, Brooke?" he asks with a grin on his face.

"Can you go unload the truck that just pulled up? We need to get the bar restocked." I wiggle my eye brows at him hoping he will do it. I know he will, but I like messing with him.

"You know all you had to do was say was 'hey Ryan, go unload that truck.'" He wiggles his eye brows back at me, crossing his arms over his chest.

"You know I love you, Ryan," I say as I smile at him. Without Ryan coming back, I wouldn't be able to get anything done. Tic has been amazing too, but Ryan has stood by my side and done anything I've asked of him.

"I love you too," he says, turning and leaving the room.

I stand from the desk and head out into the main room to make sure all the chairs are set up. A few of the girls opted to return, but a few didn't want to. I can't say that I blame them either. Tic stepped in there, too. He called in some girls he knows, and they were all amazing. I did turn Thursday night into man's night, and I think I may have talked Tic into stripping – at least a few times. It was funny to see his face when I asked him. He had this cocky ass grin that said he would outdo everyone else I hired. The girls liked the idea, too. It wasn't my dream to own a female strip club, but I'm making it work.

Overall I think the club looks really good. We got all the new permits in place with my name on them. I got the liquor licenses, too. I was surprised by all the work that had to go into starting up the club. My uncle clearly had his hands full.

"You strippin' tonight?" That deep, sexy voice booms through the room. I turn on my booted heel and smile when I see him.

"No, but I have a spot for you on Thursdays." Mayhem grins at me before stepping closer. He grabs me, pulling me into a hug.

"Missed you lately," he says softly.

My heart does a little flip in my chest. I've grown to have a soft spot for this man. "Missed you, too. I've been really busy."

He pulls back, looking around the club, but never letting me go.

"I can see that. It looks great in here. Tic's boys are good," he says as he checks out the room.

"They have been amazing. Hey, do you know when Blu will be around? I need to talk to him. I know he put the money in the account." Mayhem raises his eyebrows like he's going to deny it, but I know Blu did it.

"Havin' a party tonight for Cherry's birthday. You should come by. It'd be nice to hang out a while." he says casually. I watch the look in his eyes. I know there's more.

"What? What is it, Mayhem? Don't hold back," I tell him.

He lets out a long sigh before he says, "He looks like shit. This shit's hittin' him hard, Brooke. He misses you. The motherfucker is just too stubborn to admit it."

I give him a soft smile. I miss him too, but that part of my life is over. I need to move forward.

"He didn't want me. We both knew it would end at some point. I may come by and talk to Blu later, though. I really need to know what percentage he wants for the club." I thought at first I'd be pissed when I realized that Blu had added money to the club account, but the more I looked at what I took to run this place, the more I realized I needed the help.

"I doubt it'll be much. He just wanted you on your feet."

I reach toward the bar and grab the bottle of Jack sitting there. "Come celebrate with me," I tell him, stepping out of his grasp.

"You got it! Line it up, darlin'."

I pull the glasses out from behind the bar and fill them up. We might as well get wasted. Mayhem and I drink like it will be our last drink ever. We knock back more than we should, but we're laughing and having a good time.

"Shit! I gotta back. Want me to drop you off at home?" Mayhem asks, looking at the clock. Shit. I need to go meet Ash, too.

"Yes! I was supposed to meet Ash at her house an hour ago." I giggle. Mayhem grabs my hand and leads me toward the back door when I see Ryan.

"You sure you got tonight?" I ask him. He nods his head.

"You know it. I'll call if we need anything."

Mayhem passes me his helmet and watches as I slide it on. Once he's satisfied, he takes off down the road. I throw a wave goodbye to Ryan, safe in knowledge that my club is in good hands.

It's weird riding with him. I've only been on Dec's bike. The feeling is off with Mayhem in front of me.

Before I know it, he pulls up in front of Ash's and lets me off.

"Thanks for the ride!" I giggle softly, having had a few too many drinks at the club.

"See you in a bit!" he calls out before taking off. I turn to head toward the door when Ash comes out. She watches me intently before crossing her arms over her chest.

"What are you doing?" she asks me.

"Nothing. Mayhem came by the club and brought me home. We had a few drinks."

She smiles at me before the words leave her mouth. "Truth or dare, Brooke."

I narrow my eyes at her. What the hell is she doing? "Dare," I tell her.

She grins at me and says, "I dare you to go get a beer from the bikers."

Chapter 45

Declan

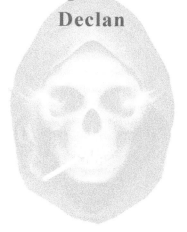

"Gimme another one, Cherry Bear," I say when she leans into the cooler to grab a beer. She smiles and grabs me out another.

"You ok, Dec?" she asks as I pop the top off and take a long pull.

"I'm ok. You havin' a good party?" I ask her. The guys went all for her. This is one hell of a party. They always do for her, though. Cherry may be a club whore, but they respect her for what she does for the club. She keeps it cleaned and in order. She deserves a good night.

"Yeah. It's nice. I wish she was here, though. I miss her," she says, picking at the label of her bottle.

"I didn't mean for shit to turn bad between the two of you," I admit. When Brooke left me, she left us all. Except for Tic, of course.

"It wasn't your fault, Declan, and I get why she doesn't come around. I can't say that I blame her. It has to be hard on her, too. I just miss her is all. She was always nice to me." I pull Cherry into my side before I sigh.

"I know. But you know she just lives down the road. You can always go see her." Cherry shakes her head before looking up at me.

"No. It feels like I'm betraying the club somehow. Does that even make sense?" Cherry has always been this way. She never liked feeling like she did something that could piss someone off here. This is different, though. My phone rings in my pocket. I slide it out and see it's Mouse.

"What?" I growl into the phone.

"We got a problem out here at the gate," he says. I tip my head back and let out a breath.

"I'm comin'." I click the end button and look down at Cherry. "Got a problem at the gate.

I'll be back." I kiss her cheek and jump off the table I'd been sitting on.

Walking toward the gate, I get a strange feeling in the pit of my stomach. Mouse stands there with his arms crossed over his chest, and I lift my chin when he looks back over at me.

"What the fuck is goin' on?" I ask him. He shakes his head, stepping to the side. I watch his face as I walk out of the gate and see her standing there.

"This little girl here is tryin' to get a beer," Mouse says. I can sense the smile on his face as I stare at her.

"That so?" I cross my arms over my chest.

Brooke stands there looking as gorgeous as ever.

"Yeah. She said it was some kind of dare," Mouse chimes in.

"Go up to the cooler and bring me a beer, Mouse." I don't move as he walks away. I stand there, watching her like a hawk.

"What are you doin' here?" I ask her. God, how I want to grab her and pull her into me. Kiss her like she's never been kissed before. I fucking want her pinned up against the wall taking my dick like she's never taken it before.

"I was dared to come get a beer from the bikers," she says shyly.

"You gonna do that thing with your tongue if I give you one?" I ask her. She gives me a slight smile before taking a step back.

"I'm sorry, Declan. I really am." She turns on her heel and starts to walk away. Her ass moving so fucking deliciously in her skin-tight jeans.

"I didn't tell you to leave," I growl.

Brooke stops walking and lets her head drop forward. I move toward her, my heart thundering inside of me. I feel like I might pass out, like a fucking kid about to get a piece of candy.

"I didn't want to fuck your life up any more than I already did, butterfly." I rest my hand on her shoulder, and God help me, that's all it takes. I want her. I want inside of her. I want her next to me. It's always like this with us.

"How could you? I'm the one that fucked up your life. I brought all my bullshit to your doorstep," she says. I don't miss the sob that escapes her, either. I spin her around so she has to look up at me.

"I wanted your bullshit. I craved it, Brooke. You made me tick. You made me want to fuckin' breath. Then you were gone. It was like everything I've ever felt was ripped away from me." She wipes at her eyes.

"I feel the same thing, Dec."

"You with Tic now?" I asked needing to know.

"What?" She looks shocked when I ask her that.

"You two been spendin' a lot of time together. He always comes back here lookin' happy." Her face looks surprised by my statement.

"Are you kidding me? She's been after him behind my back and didn't say anything? I thought those two were acting a little funny together. It certainly explains a lot," she says more to herself than me. I'm a little lost here, having no idea who or what she was referencing.

"Is that a no?"

"No! Declan, I don't want Tic. He's been a good friend, and he's helped me so much with the club. That's it! Oh my God, I can't even believe you'd think that I would fuck Mayhem before I would Tic." She laughs.

"I'll take you up on that!" I glance over my shoulder and see Mayhem standing there with two beers in his hands.

"The fuck you will!" I roar. The laughter from Brooke stops, but Mayhem has a smile plastered across his face.

"Mouse said you wanted a beer." He steps around me and passes one to Brooke. She takes it with a smile. A smile I want to be mine.

"I can't do this shit," I mumble. I can't watch her being happy with someone else. It's fucking killing me. She smiles at him and cries with me. It's too much.

I turn to walk away when she says, "I love you, Declan. Only you. I like the feel of hard steel between my legs." Those words. Those are the words she said to me that first night. I slowly turn to look at her. She smiles before passing her beer back to Mayhem. She closes the space between us quickly. Her hands rest on my chest.

"You're all I've ever wanted, Declan. From the first time you touched me, something felt real in my life. You were real."

Chapter 46

Brooke

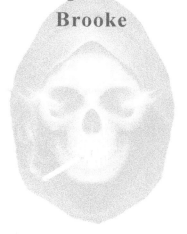

I talked to Blu. He wanted to help with the club, and I more than appreciated it. We worked out all the details, and overall, it's better for me with the Soulless Bastards being a part of it.

"Why is the club called Soulless Bastards?" I ask Declan. He looks down at me and shrugs.

"We've always been soulless," he says.

"You have a heart though, all of you do," I tell him.

He nods before he says, "Hearts, yeah. It doesn't say heartless bastards." He laughs, and it's like music to my ears. I've missed him. Missed this.

I watch Cherry dance and have a good time at her party. She deserves it. She's a good person with a good heart.

"The guys missed you around here," Declan says. I lean into his touch. Loving the way he feels against me.

"I've missed them too. Tic is nice and all, but he can be a handful. He bosses everyone around." I giggle a little. I remember him bossing the damn boss of the construction company.

"He's a good guy, though. Mayhem has been bitchin' and whinin' about you comin' back."

"He was? He's the one that came to pick me up at the club." I look up when I hear that rumble in Declan's chest. I can see the way his eyes jerk around to find Mayhem. The anger of his jealousy amuses me.

"He did, huh?"

"That growly caveman thing you do is kind of sexy," I tease him. Declan laughs before he pulls me into his lap. I stand up and spin around, straddling him.

"You like when I'm all caveman, huh?" he says, tucking a piece of hair behind my ear. His fingers graze my skin, and that's all it takes. My body shutters every time he touches me.

"I need you, Declan. I never thought that I would need anyone in my life. I was always left to fend for myself but you, I can't seem to shake the feelings I have for you." It's hard for me to admit that, but it's the truth.

"Come on." He pushes me off his lap before he stands and grabs my hand. He drags me through the crowd of people and out into the road. He doesn't stop though. He keeps walking.

My heart races when he stops at the spot.

"I've messed up so many times in my life. I killed. I still do. The world changed that night, Brooke. I looked down into your eyes and saw all the hurt and pain that I fuckin' caused you. It broke my fuckin' heart to know that I took that part of your life away from you. Every night I'd lay in bed and see your eyes. Not the eyes of the man I killed. Not the scene before me. It was you. Your eyes have haunted me since that night," he admits, staring at the exact spot where he killed my dad. My heart wants to break for him. I reach into my pocket and pull the rosary out and hand it to him. I watch as his fingers slowly move over the cross, lost in his own thoughts.

"Why did you give that to me that night?" I ask. I've always wondered about that.

"My mom gave it to me. She always said it would protect me. I wanted it to protect you. I don't know why, but when I saw the look in your eyes, I knew. You were broken by my hand. I wanted you to have somethin' good. She was good, mom was."

I reach for his hand and squeeze it in mine. "I don't even remember my mom. I was so young when she died. At least you have that memory of yours. You should keep it safe, Declan."

"Here. Keep it. You need it more than I do." He passes the rosary back to me.

"Declan." I start to protest when he spins me around. His hands come up to cup my cheeks.

"Everything I've ever wanted is all inside of you. You are what I want, Brooke. You hold my heart. I want you," he says in a demanding tone.

"You do?" I ask not sure that I heard him right.

"I love you, Brooke. I love your attitude. I love how you test my patience. I love how you snore lightly in your sleep. Fuck, there's nothin' about you that I don't love." Before I can open my mouth, Declan closes it with his.

His lips are on mine, and everything else just fades away. Nothing matters in this moment but him. He makes me feel whole. He makes me feel loved and cared for. When he pulls back, I smile up at him.

"You're lucky I love you or I'd kick your ass for manhandling me like that." Declan throws his head back and laughs a real, deep laugh.

"Come on, we got a party to get to." Declan drags me down the road again, only this time I'm high on him.

We walk back into the party when everyone turns to face us.

"I'm only gonna say this one more time," Declan hollers. Everyone settles down, and all eyes are on us.

I look up at Declan and try to get a read on what it is he's doing when he says, "Brooke's my old lady. For now and forever. I'm claimin' her ass one last time!" he roars. The guys all go crazy. Mayhem moves toward me first, lifting me in his arms and spinning me around.

"Told you, you are family! You're stuck with us now!" he laughs.

When he sets me down, Cherry runs toward me.

"I'm so happy for you, Brooke. You deserve to be happy," she squeals in my ear.

I hold her tightly before I say, "Happy Birthday!" She smiles when she pulls back. Blu is standing there watching me.

"This mean you're stayin' this time?" His tone is harsh like always. Dec moves back to my side, grabbing my hand in his.

"I think you're stuck with me," I tell Blu. He nods once before stepping forward.

"He went through hell for you. It ate him alive. I watched him spiral downward the last few months, and I hated it. He's like a son to me. We're brothers. I know you two had your reasons, but love is stronger than the shit we deal with." I get what he's saying. He doesn't want me to hurt Declan anymore, and I don't plan on it.

"I get it, Blu. You guys mean a lot to me. I love Declan." He nods before pulling me into a hug.

"I'm glad you're back, Brooke," he whispers in my ear.

When he pulls back, he says, "We still have that issue with Mouse and you kickin' his ass!" He points at me. I try not to laugh. It isn't funny. I disrespected the club and Mouse, and I feel like shit for it.

"I'm really sorry I did that. I wasn't trying to be an ass." Blu starts laughing and so does Declan. I look around at them a little confused.

"I ain't mad at you, darlin'. Mouse did his job. He knew better than to lay a hand on a woman, but nevertheless, he got his ass handed to him. We're gonna give him hell for that," Blu says as he walks away laughing.

Declan grabs me around the waist and leads me to the side of the clubhouse. Standing in the darkness of the shadows, he pulls his gun from the back of his jeans. He settles it on my chest before dragging it farther down.

"Now, butterfly. You want that hard steel between your thighs?" he asks, rubbing his gun between my legs and setting all my senses on fire.

"I want your hard steel between my thighs. I love you, Dec."

"I love you, butterfly."

Did you enjoy Declan, Soulless Bastards MC? Keep in mind that this is just the NoCal Chapter's series. There will be more to come! Stick around and watch for Mayhem's story next!

Like always, if you enjoyed this book please leave a review. Come stalk me on facebook at Erin M Trejo. Like my author page! Join my reader group, Fire and Ice.

CPSIA information can be obtained
at www.ICGtesting.com
Printed in the USA
BVHW03s0757071018
529495BV00001B/85/P

9 781723 099731